BIRGIT VANDERBEKE

TRANSLATED FROM THE GERMAN BY
JAMIE BULLOCH

Peirene

Ich freue mich, dass ich geboren bin

AUTHOR

One of Germany's most successful authors, Birgit Vanderbeke was born in Dahme, East Germany, in 1956. When she was six her family fled to the West and she grew up in Frankfurt. She has written twenty-one novels and won five prestigious literary awards, including the Ingeborg Bachmann Prize and the Kranichstein Literary Prize.

TRANSLATOR

Jamie Bulloch has worked as a literary translator from German since 2007. His works include books by Robert Menasse and Timur Vermes. He is the translator of five Peirene titles: *Portrait of the Mother as a Young Woman*, *Sea of Ink*, *The Mussel Feast*, *The Empress and the Cake* and *The Last Summer*.

Jamie Bulloch translation of Birgit Vanderbeke's novel *The Mussel Feast* won the 2014 Schlegel-Tieck Prize and was shortlisted for the 2014 Independent Foreign Fiction Prize, receiving a special mention from the jury. He is also the author of *Karl Renner: Austria*.

MEIKE ZIERVOGEL
PEIRENE PRESS

Today, as in the past, people flee
from one country to another
in the hope of finding a better
future. But how do children
experience such displacement?
How do they cope with the
traumas of a refugee camp?
In this novel Birgit Vanderbeke
goes back to her own childhood
in the divided Germany of
the 1960s. She shows how
the little girl she once was
saved herself by imagining
countries on the far side of
the world. A masterpiece of
memory turned into fiction.

First published in Great Britain in 2019 by
Peirene Press Ltd
17 Cheverton Road
London N19 3BB
www.peirenepress.com

First published under the original German language title *Ich freue mich, dass ich geboren bin* by Piper Verlag GmbH, München
Copyright © 2016 Piper Verlag GmbH, München/Berlin

This translation © Jamie Bulloch 2019

With special thanks to Gesche Ipsen, who edited *You Would Have Missed Me* for Peirene.

ISBN 978-1-908670-52-6

Designed by Sacha Davison Lunt
Cover image: simpleinsomnia Flickr/CC 2.0
Typeset by Tetragon, London
Printed and bound by T J International, Padstow, Cornwall

The translation of this work was supported by a grant from the Goethe-Institut

GOETHE INSTITUT

BIRGIT VANDERBEKE

TRANSLATED FROM THE GERMAN BY
JAMIE BULLOCH

Peirene

You Would
Have Missed Me

History is denial in narrative form;
war history is concoction for the purpose of
repetition. It always begins with a failure
to recognize reality.

— GERHARD ZWERENZ

We have our best ideas between the ages of five and ten. Some people have only a few ideas after that, maybe until they're twenty-five or thirty, depending on whether they're still talking to anyone then, but after thirty most of them no longer want to talk to anyone, they've given up, so obviously that puts an end to any more ideas.

I had my best idea when I was seven, because at the time I urgently needed to talk to someone, and when it occurred to me how I might go about that I sensed too that it was a really good idea, although I didn't realize quite how good until much later.

To be precise, it happened on my seventh birthday.

We were standing in our two-bedroom flat in the Promised Land and once again it was clear that I wouldn't be getting a cat for my birthday.

I'd been wanting a kitten ever since we left the refugee camp. I was five back then. This was the third birthday in a row I wouldn't be getting one.

You get used to disappointments, but in the long term they make you feel cold and empty inside, and you begin to lose heart.

*

It wasn't true that pets were banned in the new housing development.

The Egners in 24C had a dachshund in their first-floor flat, and Gisela's mother bred chinchillas in the basement. Everybody knew, and nobody had yet raised any objections to the Egners' dachshund or Gisela's mother's chinchillas. The chinchillas lived in cages like the rabbits at Grandma's, but Grandma was in the East. Sometimes she'd kill one of her rabbits, usually on a Friday before her sons came to visit. On the Saturday they'd be skinned and would then appear on the table on Sunday and be eaten.

Now we were in the West and things were done differently. Gisela's mother didn't kill her chinchillas and didn't skin them for a roast, but very soon she'd be selling them live to a furrier, which would make her rich, because the furrier would kill and skin the animals, then pay her 300 marks per fur. That was a lot of money for Gisela's mother, but the price would go even higher, to 400 or 500 marks, definitely. At least that's what Herr Reiland said, who'd sold Gisela's mother her first chinchillas, a pair for 2,000 marks, and since then those chinchillas had been reproducing as quickly as Grandma's rabbits in the East. Four times a year. Soon the basement wouldn't be big enough for her breeding programme, but then the family would move anyway, because they'd be so rich they wouldn't know what to do with all that money, so rich that they'd be able to afford their own bungalow. Gisela's mother wouldn't have to work part-time as a cleaner any more and her father wouldn't have to work night shifts at the red factory and sleep during the day when Gisela and her sister wanted to listen to Elvis Presley on the radio.

None of this was a secret. Everyone knew. And so, when my mother said we weren't allowed to have a cat on the estate, it wasn't true and my mother too knew perfectly well it wasn't true. This was one of those things I couldn't bear about most adults: they lied all the time.

Whenever you said anything, no matter what it was, either they didn't listen or they told you lies because they thought you were too small to realize you were being lied to, and in any case the estate's management wouldn't have objected, it was just that my mother didn't want me to have a cat, but she didn't say why.

It was my birthday, so we were standing in the lounge instead of sitting in the kitchen as usual. We only really spent time in the lounge when there was something to watch on television or if it was a special occasion. It was stuffed with teak furniture, as much as could fit inside the room. Both my father and my mother now said that it had been a mistake to furnish the lounge with teak because teak needed to be polished all the time to keep it shiny.

Before we came to the West my mother had always dreamed of teak furniture, but of course she didn't know you had to polish teak all the time because she'd only ever dreamed of it and had never owned any.

Her teak dream harked back to her fiancé, who she always claimed had been killed in action, but actually he'd been shot in the back and died. After the war everything fell apart for a few years, but you would have thought that by now things would have been slowly pieced back together, however this fiancé had been the son of a land-owner and if he hadn't been shot he would have undoubt-edly married my mother after the war, and later the two of them and their children would have inherited his family estate furnished from top to bottom with teak, and so ever since her engagement to the landowner's son my mother had dreamed of teak furniture, and as soon as my parents' application for a flat in the West was approved and we moved from the refugee camp into the housing development that the red factory had built for its workers, their first purchase was a complete teak suite for the lounge, because my mother had been dreaming of this for so long.

In fact we had many valuable things my mother could only have dreamed of in the East. We had a fridge, a washing machine, an electric cooker with four rings and an oven below, a coffee machine and even a bread-slicer, plus a master bedroom with a double bed, a wall unit made of birch wood and two bedside tables, everything in matching colours and brand new; we had a television set and we had a car, which in the East my mother could have spent a hundred years dreaming about because that was how long she'd have had to wait before being able to afford one, and then it would only have been a Trabant or at best a Wartburg, but not an Opel Kapitän.

In the Promised Land you could buy everything you dreamed of straight away, even if you couldn't immediately afford it: carpets, satin curtains, gold-rimmed crockery, crystal rummers, an ESGE hand blender, the birch-wood bedroom unit and all the teak my mother had been dreaming of since the war and the relationship with her fiancé, and which would have remained a dream if we hadn't fled, because after the war there was none of that in the East. All they get there is plastic and elastic, my father used to say.

Although it wasn't every day that my mother told the story about the teak furniture and her fiancé, she did come out with it now and again, and once you'd heard and thought about it a few times, you realized that it was quite thorny.

There were a few thorns that put my father into a bad mood, but rather than talk about them he would merely vent his bad mood and that wasn't pleasant. At times it could get really dangerous, and even if you had a rough idea of what had put him in a bad mood that didn't help; it was still dangerous.

That's why I urgently needed an idea.

Sometimes he did respond, when my mother told the story of her fiancé. For example:

May I remind you that, first of all, this son of a landowner is dead and he'd most certainly be bald by now?

My father was still quite young and, besides, he had black hair. Only men with blond hair go bald.

Then he went on to say that, second, the country estate wouldn't have amounted to much even if her fiancé hadn't been bumped off, because everything his family owned would have been expropriated after the war, and then life wouldn't have been quite so rosy, even if they hadn't been Nazis, but because they *were* Nazis, like all landowners and fat cats, I don't suppose they would have had much to laugh about under the Russians. My father would usually add that, by the way, he thought this was perfectly fair.

May I also point out that you lost the war? he concluded. He mostly said this very softly and quietly, the way he always spoke when he was really angry.

Sometimes he didn't fancy being really angry and then he'd conclude by telling my mother, you're an old Nazi and always will be. Usually my mother would start crying at that. Nobody knew why, even though I could think of a few reasons, and my father would whistle that song in which the girl desperately wants her young beau to get her an edelweiss flower. It takes place somewhere in the mountains, the boy climbs up the steep rock face, intent on plucking an edelweiss, then loses his grip, falls and dies up there. A vile song that always filled me with horror and ended with the girl forever running to his grave because there lay the only friend she'd ever had.

My mother pulled out her handkerchief, which was wedged between her blouse and waistband, and wiped her face. Then she said, you don't understand, Osch, and my father said, that's how it is, but don't keep calling me Osch.

My father didn't like it when people called him Osch. In the East everyone apart from his mother had called him

14

Osch. She'd called him *dommen jong*, silly boy, which he didn't like either, but he preferred it to Osch.

Later, when he'd turned on the television and Eintracht Frankfurt were playing Hertha, or Borussia Mönchengladbach were playing Schalke, my mother would explain to me in the kitchen that my father couldn't understand because he was too young and, besides, he wasn't German. My father was a foreigner because his mother had brought him to Germany from Belgium when he was very small and the war had already begun. Nobody knew why; his mother didn't talk about it and besides she couldn't speak a word of German, but in any event they weren't German, which means I wasn't a proper German even though I'd never been to Belgium, but you take after your father. Except my father took after his mother because when she came to Germany from Belgium she didn't bring a father for the child.

I thought the story about the teak furniture was quite thorny too, but there was no point in talking to my mother about it because she was already unhappy with the furnishings in our flat. After we'd got the teak furniture she discovered that teak is weirdly colourless; even if you constantly clean it and polish it like crazy it just remains colourless and dull, whereas my mother wanted it to look like the furniture in her fiancé's manor house, which she recalled having a warm red shimmer. Might it not have been teak after all, but larch instead?

What do you think, Osch, she asked my father, might it have been larch? Doesn't larch have that lovely warm colour? My father's hands were thrust deep in his trouser pockets, so you couldn't see them, but I knew that he was clenching his fists.

From my perspective the thorny issue of this story was quite simple: I wouldn't be here if the landowner fiancé hadn't died, but I could hardly mention this to my parents because they didn't want to talk about it and I wasn't exactly the child they'd dreamed of. I'm sure my father hadn't dreamed of any child, and then got one by accident because my mother had dreamed of a child – not the child I became, but quite a different one. I expect my mother would have been very happy if things in the war had gone differently and she could have been spared having a child so late, because if history had turned out differently she would have given birth, many years earlier and in timely fashion, to a couple of well-bred landowner children and wouldn't have had to bother with my father at the eleventh hour to avoid becoming an old spinster, and my father could have finished school in peace and then had fun studying in East Berlin with masses of girlfriends, going with them to Western cinemas, if this child hadn't got in the way. And so I kept the matter to myself, just sometimes imagined what things would have been like if I'd never been born. It wasn't quite that simple, but basically it would have been better for everyone if I'd never been born.

I could have done with somebody to talk this over with.

In the refugee camp I had Auntie Eka, Uncle Grewatsch and Uncle Winkelmann. It was worth talking to them because, even though they were very old, they were different from everyone else, but before we got on to the really important questions they were allocated a flat, as were we, and it didn't surprise me that they disappeared from our life straight afterwards because my mother couldn't stand them in the camp. It's disgusting how the three of them carry on, she used to say. At their age.

When we were in the refugee camp my father didn't live with us to begin with because he wanted to finish his studies in East Berlin and have time to think about whether he'd rather take a job in the East than join us in the West. He studied, had loads of girlfriends, like all students, and went to Western cinemas, which meant it took him a good while to decide, and so in the meantime we were in the camp without him and sometimes, if my mother didn't know what to do with me, I was allowed to visit Auntie Eka and her men, but at some point my father joined us and as soon as he was there I usually had to be there too, so that my mother could take care of me. She would clean my nose with her handkerchief and some spit, or pour warm oil into my ears if I had earache, and she would put thick mittens on my hands at night to prevent me from sucking my thumb – but also to show my father just how busy she was with me. From the day my father arrived she didn't want me to visit Auntie Eka, Uncle Grewatsch and Uncle Winkelmann any more and so she said, it's disgusting how the three of them carry on. I don't want you going over there any more, do you hear me?

Naturally, I didn't understand what could be so disgusting about the three of them all of a sudden: their room was so nice, Uncle Winkelmann had lots of books and other interesting things.

Best of all I liked the glass ball where it snowed inside. It was a magic ball. Sometimes I was allowed to give it a shake and when the snow had settled Uncle Winkelmann would say, look, it's snowing in Chengdu. Chengdu is in China. Or it's snowing in Paris, or Baghdad, and depending on where it was snowing, Uncle Winkelmann would tell me what it was like there, in Chengdu, Baghdad or Paris, because before the war he'd been everywhere and in every city on which the snow fell inside the dome.

First he went all over the world, then he was in the war, even in Russia and Italy, and finally he only just avoided capture in Italy by fleeing and defecting to the Poles, but then he ended up in Siberia.

Auntie Eka didn't like him talking about this because she was happy that the war was over, and instead of being in a Siberian camp he was now in this one with her and Uncle Grewatsch, but if you fled during the war you were a coward and shot by your own people. Fleeing keeps you busy your whole life. Although Uncle Winkelmann wasn't shot for defecting to the Poles, they handed him over to the Russians and so he went to Russia, even though he'd been there before.

All of this took place at Monte Cassino, which is in Italy. Uncle Winkelmann often talked about it because he was mulling over the question of whether he really had been a coward. The story included a monastery with monastery treasures, monks and a whole host of other things, but apart from the monks and monastery treasures I couldn't remember any details because Auntie Eka kept interrupting him, then she'd shake her long grey hair this way and that until Uncle Grewatsch said, if you don't stop that you'll end up whinnying.

Sometimes they took me into the fields to steal apples or potatoes, or they'd warm up milk with their immersion heater, and it went on like that until my father arrived at the camp and I wasn't allowed to go and see them any more. At first I couldn't understand why, but in time it came out that my mother couldn't stand Auntie Eka because she had two men.

When Auntie Eka was young, my mother said, it was indecent for her to have two men because each woman was entitled to only one man. If she's got two she's lewd and the whole thing is indecent, or at least it is so long as they're all still young. When they get older, approaching fifty, it's not indecent any more, it's simply despicable and repulsive. That's roughly what I understood my mother to be saying, and it was particularly disgusting in the camp because the three of them were living together in one room.

Everyone apart from the camp director shared rooms in the camp – the Germans were mostly three or four to a room, the Romanians and Bulgarians were often six or seven to a room, but usually these were parents with their children, not three adults. After my father's arrival things didn't look good; only seldom could I visit Auntie Eka, Uncle Grewatsch and Uncle Winkelmann, and then just in secret. Over time I realized I was losing heart and felt cold and empty inside, and of course they disappeared from our life the moment we had our own flat in the Promised Land and the question of the furniture and other valuable things arose.

As soon as the furniture company had delivered the teak suite and arranged it in our new lounge my mother knew she'd chosen the wrong furniture, and she was likewise suddenly able to remember the posh fir green of the Opel Admiral that had belonged to her landowner family.

That was quite something, she said: a dark-green Admiral.

My father said nothing because, although we didn't have the money to pay for it, we were able to buy the Opel Kapitän straight away. That didn't mean that we got it for free, because even in the Promised Land you didn't get anything for nothing, you had to pay something every month for those things that you wanted, and for the Opel Kapitän my parents had to go on paying for several years.

After a while my mother said, that was quite something before the war, a fir-green Opel Admiral.

Our Opel Kapitän was only dark blue and from after the war, and an admiral was higher up than a captain. I knew this from Uncle Winkelmann, who'd travelled the world by sea and had explained that on ships it always went from top to bottom. At the top was the admiral, then the commodore, and after that came the captain, lieutenant, sergeant and seaman.

A captain after the war couldn't compete with an admiral from before the war, that much was obvious, and it wasn't just the colour of the furniture and the cars that wasn't right in the Promised Land, rather one thing led to another, because before the war everything was good, even though my father couldn't possibly know this as he'd still been a child, and after the war everything was in ruins and broken and had to be rebuilt, and of course they rebuilt the East far more shoddily than the West because after the war the Russians had stolen and carried off everything that wasn't nailed down, as the Russians had nothing themselves, and so you could barely find a single brick for reconstruction anywhere in eastern Germany because the Russians were even poorer sods and had even less than the Germans.

But now we were in the West and we had the Americans, who hadn't stolen and carried off anything, instead they'd given us things to enable the country to look sort of tip-top again, although of course an Opel Kapitän couldn't compete with a pre-war Admiral, that was something you could only dream about.

*

Dreaming, however, was absolutely fine in the Promised Land. The wonderful thing about this country was that as soon as my mother had acquired the teak furniture and the Opel Kapitän and was disappointed because they weren't exactly what she'd been dreaming of, she could immediately start dreaming of larch furniture and an Opel Admiral, and if she acquired these and they didn't turn out to be as red or fir green as the furniture and pre-war Admiral at her landowner fiancé's house, she could simply keep dreaming. I knew this because it didn't happen only to my mother, it happened to more or less everyone, and the dreams never stopped, they just kept multiplying, because Gisela's mother spoke about her bungalow all the time, and the swing seat they'd put in the garden behind the bungalow, while the Egners or the Geisingers or the Höppners or whoever on the new estate dreamed of driving their Ford Taunus or Mercedes on holiday to the Salzkammergut or Italy, and when they'd finally been there they invited all the neighbours over to look at the photographs and slides showing them standing around in the Salzkammergut or in Italy, waving at the camera, and as soon as they'd been on holiday the next time they invited all the neighbours over again, but this time rather than photographs or slides there were shaky films, because they'd bought a Super 8 camera, and so everyone else began dreaming of bungalows or the Salzkammergut, of Italy and Super 8 cameras they could wave at, and very often my father would clench his fists in his trouser pockets because he was still young.

Or at least my mother said he was still young, he said it less often than she did, but occasionally he said it too.

I'm basically watching myself wasting my youth, he said.

What he meant by that, I think, was that he was stuck on a new estate with his unsatisfied wife and abortive child, having to watch the neighbours – who he met every day on the stairs anyway – standing around waving in the Salzkammergut. As far as my father was concerned, there was nothing promising about this land. He never said what exactly he understood by 'promise', but, livid as he was, my father smoked tons of HB cigarettes to avoid exploding with rage, although that didn't help, he was still livid, and my mother and I imagined that for him 'promise' was his East Berlin student life with the Western cinemas and girlfriends rather than the life we were living here on the new estate, even if the Americans had brought us freedom as well as money, but my father's understanding of freedom didn't necessarily include the Salzkammergut and a Super 8 camera.

I see freedom as something else, he said. He clenched his fists in his trouser pockets and clamped his teeth together so tightly that his jaw muscles moved back and forth and you could hear his teeth grinding, and I could be sure that things would soon take an unpleasant turn. Now, on my seventh birthday, it looked very much as if things would soon take an unpleasant turn, but it was my birthday and given what I knew and how birthdays had panned out in previous years, I could be fairly sure that nothing would happen today, but something might over the next few days.

Birthdays were special.

The day before, my mother had been in despair because I was a bad girl. That evening she'd told my father that she didn't know what to do with their child. My father didn't really want to listen because he'd heard it before and instead of hearing all today's details again he'd rather read the newspaper or watch the regional news, but my mother couldn't cope with their child's misbehaviour. I'm really doing all I can, she said, but there comes a time when a mother is powerless.

During the course of the day she usually got to the point where a father's hand was needed, because even with the best will in the world there was nothing more she could do after a certain juncture and then only a father's hand would help. She kept mentioning a father's hand until he started grinding his teeth and it all kicked off.

What am I to do with you? she said, and I didn't know the answer.

Sometimes I thought my father didn't know either and simply did it to stop my mother from going on about not knowing what to do and my needing a father's hand, which my father had never experienced because my grand-mother Maria had come to Germany from Belgium with only her child, and without its father.

Oh, Osch, my mother would say when my father wanted to read the paper or watch the regional news. Oh, Osch, you missed out on that, a father's hand.

Then my father would get really irate and the regional news would flicker away without him, and sometimes also the national news that followed.

This is simply how it was, and it was unavoidable. I'd have loved to have been a good little girl, but I couldn't be, and it was demoralizing trying to be a good little girl all the time without ever succeeding. Bad things were forever happening that I couldn't prevent; it was as if I were jinxed. The cup smashes, the glass falls over, the pen makes a mess, and then you're lucky if the inkblot is only in your exercise book and not on your clean blouse, and you can't help it if you fall, scrape your knee and get a hole in your tights when skipping, you can't help it if others see what knickers you've got on when you do cartwheels by the clothes line because you have to wear skirts and aren't allowed to put on trousers, and once again you've messed up, and if you've pretty much managed a whole day from morning till evening without falling over or smashing a cup, then at the very last moment you might just forget to wash your hands before supper. At any rate, there isn't a day in the year when you have the slightest chance of being a good little girl because you're plain bad.

Only on your birthday are all your crimes briefly forgotten, only then do they act as if you were a ray of sunshine in their life who has never once got up to any mischief.

Most of all, they would be delighted about the presents they'd kept hidden in their birch-wood bedroom wall unit. Only some of my presents were a surprise, one of them was always Wolfi the baby doll, with a new head. My mother wanted me to play with a baby doll and learn how to change a baby, rock it to sleep and give it a bottle, because at some point in the future I'd get married and have children and would need to be able to do all this, and I had all manner of little tops and shirts and other clothes, but the moment I began to change Wolfi or put a top on him, his head would come off, usually falling straight on the floor and breaking, because it was a china head, and if it didn't come off immediately it would do so a little later. It never stayed intact for more than a day or two.

As a child my mother would have loved a doll with a china head because a china head on a doll was as posh as a fir-green Admiral.

I'd rather not have been given Wolfi with a new head every Christmas and birthday, because I knew that I couldn't help it: the head came off each time. Then my mother would say to my father, I really don't know what to do with the child, can you believe that the doll's head is broken again?

Whenever I said I didn't do it on purpose my father grew angry and said, it would have been better if you *had* done it on purpose.

Anyway, it didn't matter whether I broke the head – or anything else, for that matter – on purpose or by accident, and that's why I'd rather not have had the doll, but each time my mother was so pleased that the doll doctor had made Wolfi better again that I couldn't object.

Sometimes the other present was a nice surprise, unless it was a present that the other children on the estate or children of colleagues had recently been given, which my parents thought would be exactly the right present for a child of my age, and from which they hoped I might learn something, like a chemistry set, a children's dictionary, a game of Scrabble I'd be thrilled about. They'd have had a better idea if they'd bothered listening to me just once.

My father wasn't interested in such trivial matters and he could think of better ways to spend his evenings after work than listening to childish babbling. He found it irritating enough having to listen to his wife talk about how she didn't know what to do with me, but my mother would have had a better idea if she had listened to me for once, rather than claiming that cats were not allowed on the estate, even though she knew perfectly well this wasn't true.

Both of them, each in their own way, thought they didn't need to listen to me because they had a much better idea of what I was dreaming of. Much better than I did. But they were wrong.

Apart from the fact that they lied to you all the time, what also annoyed me was that most grown-ups knew everything better than their children.

It didn't annoy me, obviously, that they knew things like 96×186. We hadn't learned that at school yet, and of course parents knew the answer to 96×186 when they had to pay for their washing machine and Opel Kapitän because even in the Promised Land you didn't get anything for nothing, and children didn't know this, but that wasn't what annoyed me because only very rarely did I need to know the answer to 96 × 186 on the spot.

Yet almost every day my mother knew what I wanted and what was good for me, and if my mother knew it, then my father did too because she told him, but most of all they knew what wasn't good for me. They knew what wasn't good for me from very early on in my life, and over time it got worse rather than better because we weren't talking about thumb-sucking any more, even though that wasn't a minor thing and it had taken them ages to get me to the stage where I was just about weaned off it, but that was in the East when we lived with Grandma and they could tie my hands to the bars because in the East I was still in a cot, and later in the refugee camp too, and now it was a long time since I'd sucked my thumb, at least not when anyone was looking, because my parents said I'd get buck teeth, and right from the outset they didn't want me having buck teeth on top of everything else, so my mother would dip my thumbs in hot mustard and I had to lick off the hot mustard before I could suck my thumb again. The mustard in the East was much milder than in the West. In the West it was hotter and the mustard to stop me sucking my thumbs was extra hot. My mother tried everything to stop me from getting buck teeth, and if I picked my nose I'd get a snub nose.

If I went around in bare feet I'd get pneumonia and the pneumonia would kill me. If I went cross-eyed my eyes would stay that way and would never be normal again. If I drank tap water I'd get worms.

My mother was going to take me to the dentist about my buck teeth as soon as my new teeth had come through and then she'd tell the dentist that I needed braces because I was a thumb-sucker.

Because of the worms and the other nasty habits she couldn't wean me off, we went to see Dr Ickstadt.

Dr Ickstadt lived in Akazienweg. I liked going to Akazienweg because the acacia was my favourite tree and there were lots of them growing along the street. On the brass plaque by the surgery door it said 'Isolde Ickstadt'. I thought Isolde sounded much prettier than Dr Ickstadt and also suited her better. She had an updo and wore sunglasses, and whatever the weather she drove around in a red convertible with the top down until her updo unravelled, having been battered by the wind, or got soaked and collapsed. She always came racing along in her red cabriolet a few minutes late to her surgery, braking outside the entrance with a screech. As she got out she would laugh, but then she'd see all her patients hanging around outside the surgery and say, good grief, and her hairdo was ruined.

My mother couldn't stand Isolde Ickstadt. My mother was a teacher and impressed on her pupils the importance of punctuality in life. She said that teachers and doctors had to be role models, and that we shouldn't be surprised at how children turned out if their teachers and doctors weren't good role models.

Nothing should surprise us any more, she said, if even the doctor regularly turned up late to her own surgery.

She resented Isolde Ickstadt for being in a good mood rather than feeling guilty, but we didn't have a choice because she was the only doctor for miles around, and we had to go to see her for every little thing and wait outside the surgery, and the worst thing of all was that the doctor didn't sing from the same hymn sheet as the parents.

The family doctor should sing from the same hymn sheet as the parents, my mother said, complaining that the doctor evidently didn't care that I was badly behaved and picked my nose all the time.

In truth, she'd laughed when my mother asked her what she should do to stop me from getting a snub nose.

Rather than answer my mother, she asked me, do people still say that these days?

Then she said to herself, it's amazing what adults tell children. The same nonsense over and over again. Clearly some things never change.

And if you swallow a cherry stone you'll have a cherry tree growing out of your throat. Do you know that one too? she asked.

Really? I said. Does that happen? I was fascinated.

Never, our doctor said with a hearty laugh.

I liked her a lot, and I also liked it when she said shortly before my birthday that I had to do special exercises because there was something wrong with my right side.

She'd just wanted to check to see if I'd grown. I stood by the door to which the colourful scale was tacked and then she sat back down at her desk and said, walk slowly over here, please.

Right, she said when I got there, now turn around and go back to the door.

Finally, I had to lie on her treatment table while she carried out all manner of tests and asked whether I'd had an accident, but my mother said that I hadn't had an accident.

I'm surprised, the doctor said. It looks as if the child's had a bad fall.

My mother said I was a wild girl and she had to keep her eye on me the whole time. The moment you take your eye off this girl, she said, she goes wild. She clambers over the table and chairs and climbs barefoot up every tree like a little monkey. Take a look at her knees, she said, pointing to the plasters on my knees. We don't have a clue what to do with her.

All of a sudden the doctor looked very doctorly and was no longer laughing, but saying quite a lot of words I didn't understand.

Fracture of the hip, fracture of the femur, double fracture of the shin and a few other things besides. I remembered only the word 'fracture' because she said it three times in succession.

My mother shook her head and said she couldn't explain it, and the doctor told me that I probably had a few broken bones that hadn't fused back together very

31

well, which meant my right leg was slightly shorter than my left.

Quite a lot shorter, to be honest, she added.

She wanted to send me to a friend of hers who would do some exercises with me.

My mother said that I'd been a member of the gymnastics association ever since I'd started school, but the doctor didn't respond because she was writing a referral note.

Can you take the bus on your own yet? she asked me.

My mother shook her head again, but I said, of course, as if all I'd ever done in life was to take the bus on my own.

Isolde Ickstadt's friend lived six bus stops away from our estate and she'd do a few exercises with me, which might hurt a bit the first or second time but wouldn't later on, and then it would be a piece of cake and I wouldn't be able to stop doing these exercises on my own, morning, noon and night, because each day I'd be able to move more easily, without it hurting.

Surely you must be in pain, she said.

It's OK, I said.

Well, she said, either way the pain will be completely gone in a few weeks and you'll have two legs exactly the same length again, which means that later you can go skiing and do rock 'n' roll dancing to your heart's content, and you'll turn all the boys' heads.

And so it was agreed that I could take the bus, without my mother having a chance to object.

*

It wasn't just my parents who talked about the snub nose; the children at school mentioned it too, but it was a lie. Nonetheless they all believed that they mustn't swallow cherry stones or they'd have a cherry tree growing out of their throat, and they also believed that if you went cross-eyed you'd stay that way.

In the refugee camp Auntie Eka, Uncle Grewatsch and Uncle Winkelmann could barely stop laughing when I went cross-eyed. Going cross-eyed was fun. It was something I could do really well and nothing ever got damaged. I could do it so well that later everyone would begin to shriek in horror as soon as my eyes started to move, and then the teachers told me not to do it, my eyes would stay like that, but I knew it wasn't true because my eyes had never stayed like that. At some point it struck me that you didn't have to believe everything your parents told you, but I had no idea what I should believe and what I shouldn't.

I really needed to be able to talk to them, or someone else I could trust, but it wasn't possible because Auntie Eka and her men weren't there any more and I didn't dare to go to see Isolde Ickstadt and quiz her on all those things I desperately wanted to know about while the other patients sat outside in the waiting room, already angry that the doctor had turned up late again.

That was why I urgently needed an idea.

On my birthdays, before I got Wolfi the doll and the other presents, my parents would sing the song they always sang on birthdays, or maybe my mother sang it all on

her own while my father waited for it to finish because
he found her singing tiresome and embarrassing, and he
found this song about being born especially tiresome and
embarrassing. I thought my father was quite right not
to like this song, because pretty much the whole thing
was a pack of lies.

We're so happy you were born,

my mother sang.

My father lit a cigarette to avoid exploding with rage
and kept his mouth shut, while I thought about the song.
Uncle Winkelmann had told me all about being born.

You had to picture it roughly like this. You start off
as a transparent tadpole, swimming with all the others
who haven't been born yet and most of who will never
be born, in the great black pool of eternity somewhere
in Neverland. Then a future father comes along – an
official one, hopefully, one with a fishing permit, Uncle
Winkelmann said, giving me a wink – so he comes along
and fishes one of these tadpoles out of the dark waters.
Now, I was born in eastern Germany, so it could be a
really small river, perhaps the Dahme or the Spree, or even
a pond. In the West it might be the Rhine or the Main,
and I'm sure the Liederbach would work too, or in the
big, wide world it could be one of the oceans that Uncle
Winkelmann talked about in the refugee camp. Anyway,
you're fished out of the great black pool of eternity,
while the others stay in there, either for the time being

or for ever, and really, the number of those who stay in there and may never be fished out is huge. So many that nobody could count them.

As many as the stars, Uncle Winkelmann said, lifting me up onto the windowsill so I could see the stars, but the sun was still setting and it wasn't properly dark. All the same, I could see that there were lots and lots of stars and later, when I was able to count up to more than a hundred, if I couldn't go to sleep I would stand by the window and gaze at the night sky to see how big infinity was, and there would be as many tadpoles swimming in the black pool of eternity as there were stars in the sky, which meant it was an amazing coincidence if you were fished out of there by your own father. How you got from Neverland into your future mother's tummy was a bit of a mystery in Uncle Winkelmann's explanation, because at that point in the story Auntie Eka started to cough, but so far as I could make out you went through one of the two openings down below and then you were inside. The tummy itself is like a miniature version of the great black pool, only that every day the future mother has to eat a head of lettuce with a sweet cream dressing, which on its way to the miniature pool in her tummy is transformed into a nutritious and energy-boosting solution, and in the tummy aquarium this concentrated feed helps you grow into a real froglet and then quite a while later you come out as a little person. Strangely, you find the way out all by yourself. You see it's the same way you took to get in a few months earlier, even though you were just a tadpole, but the moment you're fished out of the great black pool of eternity you've got a flawless memory and don't have to make long calculations or look anything up in one of the many books for grown-ups that Uncle Winkelmann had. You simply know where the way out is because you're already a little person when you're fished out as a tadpole and you remember the way in and everything. As soon as you're born you forget it all, even though you do actually know it, but over time you probably forget a lot of what you did actually know when you had no idea of all the things you knew, Uncle Winkelmann said, and that's why you need all these books later on. Just to find out what you actually always knew.

There was another story about being born that Uncle Winkelmann told me in the camp, but it was about my other grandmother, obviously not about Grandma who we'd lived with in the East, but my other grandmother from Wallstrasse, who we discussed once in the camp because there were a few things about this grandmother I hadn't understood. Anyway, she was Catholic because she'd fled Belgium during the war and was called Maria. Everyone in Belgium's Catholic, Uncle Winkelmann said, and just occasionally a Catholic Maria won't have an official father for her child, but she doesn't need one because the Holy Ghost personally fishes the tadpole from the black pool of eternity and plants it in her tummy. The Holy Ghost is invisible, hovering above the black pool and watching the activity at the water's edge, and hovering above him there's nothing except for God, who watches the Holy Ghost as well as the pool from above, and sometimes the Holy Ghost gets bored and simply fishes out a tadpole for himself. He's not allowed to, but he talks his way out of trouble by saying that he only did it because the boss wanted him to, and that's how one day a Maria got the Son of God inside her tummy, but it only happens to Catholics, or at least that's how Uncle Winkelmann explained being born the Catholic way in the refugee camp, because I'd quizzed him about my Belgian grandmother, of who I knew nothing save for what Grandma had pieced together with her friends from various rumours. After I'd more or less grasped the thing about the Holy Ghost, Uncle Winkelmann said that in eastern Germany – where we came from, so this presumably included us – everyone was in fact Prussian and Protestant. Prussians and Protestants don't believe in the Holy Ghost, only in what they can see, he said, but whether it was official fathers or the Holy Ghost, I found being born astonishing at the very least. You could almost say that from the great black pool of eternity to being born it's all a miracle, and that might indeed be a reason for being so happy. It's how the song went, anyway.

We're so happy you were born.

But people aren't like that. They're not all that happy when one of them is miraculously born. They just pretend to be; at least my mother just pretended.

We're so happy you were born
and that it's your bir-hirthday today.

My mother had a terribly high voice, which soon became a squeak, and she would sing this song in such a high and squeaky voice that I thought she was about to burst into tears, and I almost burst into tears myself because suddenly I didn't know who I felt more sorry for.

The answer seemed clear: me, because once again I wouldn't be getting a kitten, and the disappointment left me feeling so cold and empty inside that I was almost sick.

In truth, however, it was the others.

My father was looking at his hands, which he always did when he found something tiresome and embarrassing, and I looked at his hands too. I even felt calm as I looked at them because it was my birthday and I assumed I had nothing to fear today. It wasn't what I normally liked doing, but while my mother sang the birthday song I looked at them very calmly, and all of a sudden it was as if I'd never seen them before, even though I'd seen them every day since my father arrived at the refugee camp and decided to watch himself wasting his youth. Anyway, I'd seen his hands so often that I never thought what peculiar hands my father had and that they weren't like the hands of the other men I knew; instead, right now, as my mother was singing the silly birthday song, they were as they had been when I first met my father. Even though I was very young then and couldn't talk.

*

Of course, I didn't know that many men when I was seven. Only Herr Grashopp, who taught 1B, and I'd been in 1B since Easter; then my two uncles, who I missed but who couldn't visit us because they lived in the East and we'd fled before I was five and now lived in the West, which those in the East could only dream of but where they could never go because there was a wall and barbed wire in between, and anybody who tried to come over to the Promised Land was shot in the back and died.

I also knew Our-Uwe. He worked in the red factory like my father and Gisela's father and almost everyone apart from Herr Grashopp and the other teachers in our school and of course our doctor. The red factory was actually called the dye factory and it didn't just manufacture red, but all colours for all manner of materials, and now they were making the materials too, and as well as materials they were making textiles and medicines, but a hundred years earlier they'd started with red and on their hundredth birthday they'd built the Centenary Hall, which looked like the giant turtles in Uncle Winkelmann's animal books. Inside, the shell looked like a huge dome. They'd also built an outdoor pool that anyone who worked in the red factory could use. You got an annual pass and if you showed it at the entrance you didn't need to buy a ticket and you could swim from March to October because the pool was heated, and if it was cold outside you couldn't see if the water was blue or green or black because it evaporated the moment it came into contact with the cold air; there was always a thick layer of white mist above it.

I thought the red factory ought to be called the yellow factory because, although it had red chimneys, what puffed out of its red chimneys was yellow and you saw much more yellow than red, but it was only sulphur and not a real dye.

Our-Uwe was the boss of the department in which my father worked, and because he was the boss my father said we should say *Guten Tag, Herr Doktor* when we bumped into him in the street, even though he wasn't a proper doctor like Isolde Ickstadt. In our flat he was simply Our-Uwe because his first name was Uwe, just like Uwe Seeler, who was our football hero. Uwe Seeler played for Hamburg, but was our football hero all the same, he was everyone's hero throughout the West and everyone called him Our-Uwe.

My father said Our-Uwe was a halfwit and a poor sod, but he was damn good at football. He played like a young god, you had to give him that, and in our flat my father called his boss Our-Uwe too, even though he was already half bald and couldn't play football like a young god. At any rate, he had these very soft, slim hands. When you shook his hand it was like sticking your fingers into blancmange.

Herr Grashopp didn't shake hands, of course, because it would have been far too much to shake the hands of all forty children in the class. He was even balder than Our-Uwe, and it was very obvious even though he combed the few remaining strands of hair above his left ear across his head to his right because they didn't cover his baldness. Herr Grashopp's hands weren't as slim as Our-Uwe's, but they were as soft. They were practically the only men I knew in the West, but I had a clear memory of my uncles' hands in the East, because they were soft too and my uncles were always using them to mess about on the piano or violin or clarinet or whatever else they got hold of when they came to visit Grandma and fetched the instruments that had been lying unused up in the attic since their father died. Their father was my grandad, even though he was already dead when I was born. He'd been a conductor. After he died Grandma put all his instruments up into the attic, and when my uncles came to visit their mother they'd bring down those instruments they fancied playing and start by just making a bit of music, but then they got more and more boisterous, wilder and jauntier, sometimes quite loud too until things were really rocking and Grandma closed the kitchen door. After lunch they messed about on the instruments with their soft hands for so long that they almost fell off their chairs laughing and had to take their fingers off the piano, saxophone or ukulele. To finish up they'd always play 'Yes! We Have No Bananas' and then their mother would get cross because she had everything in her garden – peas, cucumbers and beans – but of course no bananas. They always brought her some from Berlin. But all that was back in the East and a very long time ago. All the same, I miss them.

Not as much as Auntie Eka, Uncle Grewatsch and Uncle Winkelmann, but still quite a bit.

One day my mother fled with me. She got me out of bed at night, which was why I was barely aware of what was happening. If Grandma hadn't been asleep she would surely have said goodbye, see you soon. But perhaps she wouldn't have said that because there was little possibility that we would see her again in this life. At any rate, my mother said that she'd probably never see her mother again in this life. We took the train to Berlin and then we stayed in several refugee camps, first a transit camp called Marienfelde, where everyone who fled went. Marienfelde was in Berlin, but we were there only a short time and didn't get to see anything of Berlin, not even my father or uncles. Afterwards we took a plane to western Germany, into the Promised Land. I'd thought that the Promised Land was one large land, but that wasn't right. It was divided into several smaller lands that all had their own ideas and laws. First we went to a refugee camp somewhere in the middle, but they couldn't keep us there because only Catholic refugees were allowed to come and were given work in the area around Cologne, so we had to leave after a few months and then go to another camp that used to be a barracks and was pretty much on the border between two of the smaller lands. Maybe it belonged to one, maybe to the other, and then came the question: Seligenstadt or Hanau? Again, we had to be Catholic for Seligenstadt, but for Hanau it was OK to be Protestant or even nothing, but then we didn't go to Hanau because my father had joined us and because of my father and the red factory we moved to the housing development in Frankfurt. My mother became a teacher for the third time in her life and my father started work at the red factory.

Plastic and elastic, my mother said, because we just got a little works flat, which didn't bear the remotest resemblance to her fiancé's estate, not even to Grandma's house in the East, but my father said that the dye factory was not plastic and elastic at all, it was an international firm of global repute.

The red factory couldn't care less whether you were Catholic or Protestant. What counted at the red factory was your degree.

As far as they're concerned I could be Chinese or a Zulu, my father said after applying to the red factory, and although I'm not German, I'm not a Zulu negro either.

As far as they're concerned I could be a Zulu, he said, the key thing is my degree, and here he was in luck because he'd done his degree in East Berlin. The East German degrees were worth more than the West German ones, and of course they were worth more than the Bulgarian and Romanian ones because those were issued in Bulgarian and Romanian and nobody could read them, and anyway the red factory was happy that masses of East Germans with East German degrees had fled to the West, and the factory could help itself to as many of them as it liked, and the East Germans were happy to get work in the red factory with their degrees after having become pretty disheartened in the refugee camps, often getting drunk because they didn't know what the future held until their papers were finally stamped, and because it isn't good if men can't do anything but wait, and so finally my father started at the red factory in Our-Uwe's department, but like all refugees he started fairly near the bottom because they wanted to see how he worked first, and make sure he wasn't a Russian spy and that sort of stuff, and if he wasn't a spy he would in time surely climb the ladder.

You see, in the red factory there was a ladder. As an East German refugee you started on one of the lower rungs and then climbed up rung by rung and eventually my father might make it to that point on the ladder for which his degree said he was qualified, having learned everything in his studies that you needed to know to be quite high up. A Mercedes was quite high up in the Promised Land. A Mercedes was even better than a pre-war Admiral.

The ladder in the red factory obviously wasn't as important to me as it was to my father. I'd have been perfectly happy for us to have stayed in the refugee camp.

There were quite a lot of people in the camp, but I liked being among lots of people; at least, I preferred that to just the three of us in the small room. There were very many Bulgarian and Romanian children in the camp who were allowed to run around and play. My mother didn't want me to play outside or spend time with them, but they were there, you could hear them. In fact you could hear most things that other people did, whether they were singing or laughing or arguing or whatever. Of course, when they were loud you could hear them particularly clearly.

Sometimes it got incredibly loud in the evenings and at night. Sometimes during the day too.

First you'd hear people being loud in a room or a corridor, then after a while you'd hear a shh, either from one of the people being loud or from someone next door or above or below. Usually they'd grow quieter after that, unless they were drunk. The Bulgarians and Romanians drank slivovitz and the Germans drank beer and schnapps. They'd pour themselves a large glass of beer and a small glass of schnapps, then sink the little glass in the big one and that was called a submarine.

When it got loud in our room my mother would usually say, shh.

Or she'd say, Osch, please be quiet, everyone can hear you.

In truth both of them could be heard, and when she said, Osch, please be quiet, it was high time to make myself invisible and slip off to Auntie Eka and her men because my father hated being called Osch, and he particularly hated it if he'd been drinking submarines, and then it was usually quite a while before peace returned to our room, but as soon as I'd slipped off and was with

Auntie Eka, Uncle Grewatsch and Uncle Winkelmann I could have stayed in the camp for ever.

Uncle Grewatsch had slim hands with wrinkles, which spent most of the time in his lap. I didn't pay as much attention to Uncle Winkelmann's hands. I always had to look at Uncle Winkelmann's face because most of the time he was talking to someone, to Auntie Eka or Uncle Grewatsch or me, and when he spoke he would say something with his mouth or tell a story and his entire face would talk too, his eyes turned big or funny or sad, or they looked surprised because he didn't understand the world.

It's beyond me, he sometimes said, or he'd say, I can't help it, but the older I get the less I understand the world. Sometimes he would screw his eyes up in irritation and there were lines around his mouth, just like those on his brow. At any rate, I barely had time to look at his hands, apart from once when he was telling me about the three monkeys that stood on the table in the refugee camp among Uncle Winkelmann's mountains of books and were never put away, not even when the three of them or all of us had coffee and there was warm milk for me. Those were soft hands that lifted the three monkeys and carefully placed them back on the table, and then I was already looking at Uncle Winkelmann's face again because he was telling me about the three monkeys and I didn't want to miss a single word or a single movement of his eyes or the lines on his face, even though I didn't understand everything he said, but I did understand he was talking to me and that what he was saying was important and I resolved for the rest of my life never to stop looking or listening when something evil was happening because that would be cowardly.

Watch very carefully, Uncle Winkelmann said after he'd told me that the three monkeys were cowards.

Watch very carefully, do you hear? No matter what they tell you, listen and open your mouth. The world might have been spared a great deal.

Do you have to talk politics with the child now? Auntie Eka said, and Uncle Winkelmann said, it just slipped out, then his slim hand stroked my head as if he were trying to sweep the three monkeys away, but they were already inside my head.

Anyway, my father had very different hands from the other men I'd met and known by the time I was seven.

I knew of course that he'd been trapped in a fire when he was a child and the flames almost hadn't been put out in time. That was in the second year of the war, but it didn't have anything to do with the war, it was just wartime and he'd just accidentally been trapped in a fire at kindergarten shortly after his mother, Maria, and he had arrived in Germany and she'd sent him to kindergarten and he'd been trapped in the fire and they hadn't put the flames out until quite late and he was taken to hospital.

In hospital they said that he probably wouldn't survive, but his mother had experience of hospitals saying he wouldn't survive because they'd said that when he was born too. When he was born his umbilical cord had wrapped itself around his neck twice and he'd been blue in the face. His mother had unwound the umbilical cord, that was in Belgium, in Ostend, where she'd lived before fleeing to Germany, and then she'd asked them to call for a priest, and by the time the priest came to read the last rites to the blue infant, my grandmother had already unwound the umbilical cord and my future father had started breathing on his own. The priest had come for no reason and he was annoyed to have missed out on the last rites and the fee that went with them. The child wasn't even blue in the face any more. So when, a few years later, they told her in this German hospital that her child probably wouldn't survive his burns, my grandmother refused to give up. She asked them to call for a priest, but she said it in Belgian so nobody understood her. It wouldn't have helped if anyone had understood her as there weren't any priests in eastern Germany because they weren't Catholic there, Protestant if anything, and they weren't priests but merely Prussian pastors. So my future grandmother just stayed at her child's side and eventually he survived, but because back then they couldn't transplant skin, or any other organs for that matter, his skin didn't heal properly, it grew back the wrong way and unevenly, and that's how the boy looked afterwards when he was back on his feet again, and now, on my seventh birthday, all you could see were the two hands that my father and I were staring at while my mother sang the birthday song. I'd got used to the way his hands looked, but that day I looked at them as if I'd never seen them before and all of a sudden they didn't look the same as usual, and certainly not like Herr Grashopp's or Our-Uwe's hands, but different. They looked like the hands I'd first encountered: huge paws covered in rubbery growths.

I can't remember what it was like being born, but from what they used to tell me it seemed almost as if everything had been fine up to that point. On birthdays people sometimes try to piece together how life was before and how it all happened then, and from everything I managed to piece together on my seventh birthday, it had basically passed without any problems.

My uncles lived in Berlin; sometimes they came at the weekend and told us about the Western cinemas they went to and the films they'd seen. *Diamond Machine*, *Yours Truly, Blake*. They would come with bananas and play music in the lounge until they couldn't stop laughing, and Grandma said they were yobs and that life in the big city had ruined them for good.

Sometimes she would open the veranda window and say, one day you'll be locked up and they'll throw away the key. She also said, don't let Comrade Lamprecht hear you talking like that.

Then there would be rabbit or veal kidney chops with chanterelles and dumplings, just like later, after I was born.

They didn't take their wives to Grandma's because the women didn't want to come. One was a gypsy woman my uncle had got together with during the war when travelling the country with a circus to avoid having to go to the front. One of the circus horses was sensitive to his wild clarinet music and bit off one of his ears, but later he married the very woman who performed the stunts on the horse that had bitten off his ear.

My other uncle wasn't actually married yet, just engaged. His fiancée had arrived on a handcart from Silesia after the war and lived in Wallstrasse, where my grandmother Maria also lived. Most people who'd fled from somewhere but didn't move on to anywhere else lived in Wallstrasse, and the majority of them spent the rest of their lives there among each other. At least, that's what Grandma said, but it wasn't true because my uncle intended to marry his fiancée and then take her from Wallstrasse to Berlin and the Western cinemas. Or that's what my uncle said, but Grandma wouldn't listen.

My future mother had become a teacher during the war; after the war she had to do eight months of training because, of course, everything she'd learned before and taught the children had come from the Nazis and after the war it was outdated and no longer acceptable. Afterwards she was a 'new teacher' in the Soviet sector. She went to school and earned money, Grandma kept the house clean, cooked and baked cakes and looked after the washing, the garden, the chickens and the rabbits, and everyone was happy that the war was now a few years in the past because it had thrown everything into chaos. None of them had died apart from Grandma's husband, who'd come from Bohemia and been a conductor, but he'd come after the First World War and although he died in the Second World War he died quite normally, at Christmas, stupidly, but he died of cancer rather than the war, where you got shot in the back like my future mother's fiancé, but when I was born all of that was quite a long way in the past, and if I hadn't been born life could have gone on in much the same fashion. There weren't any bananas or films from the West, but they could get over that.

A few years after the war, however, my mother started dreaming of having a husband and a child and another life, even though she was basically fine, but she was over thirty and at her age women would start talking about her not having a husband and soon becoming an old spinster.

The moment the dream of a husband and child and another life had been planted inside my mother's head, long after her landowner fiancé was out of the picture and she could have let the matter rest – at that moment everything started to get complicated and descend into chaos.

Grandma had seen it at once, but of course there was nothing she could do about it, just as she hadn't been able to do anything about her sons, whose lives would only be made more difficult by their wives.

I knew all this because Grandma looked after me when I was born and my mother had to go back to work.

I don't have particularly clear memories of my mother from that time, because she was only around for short periods. In truth I can only remember her kissing me to the point where my face was full of her spit, then giving me to Grandma, who wiped my face and made it dry again. Grandma and I were always together and spent every day at home alone, and sometimes Grandma would talk to herself while she was cooking or in the garden and had forgotten that I was there. Perhaps she also thought that I was too small, and talked to herself because usually there was nobody else she could talk to and she'd got used to the fact that nobody talked to her, or at least she talked to herself about everything that was on her mind and so I heard that my mother and Osch would never last.

Grandma often told herself that she hadn't had an easy life and there had been lots of things she'd been unable to do anything about. She'd said yes and amen to her elder son marrying a gypsy woman from the circus, and to her younger son getting together with a girl from Wallstrasse, where that whole pack of refugees lived who'd come on carts from Silesia or Pomerania after the war with nothing in their pockets and had eaten the decent folk out of house and home.

Nor had she been able to do anything about her daughter wanting to have a different life and a child, when she already had a good life with her mother, wanting for nothing except of course for those bananas, but the uncles often brought them when they came on Sundays.

But Grandma wouldn't have been happy either if her friends had started talking about her daughter turning into an old spinster soon. Grandma had married as a very young woman. She was happy it was all behind her and that she'd been a widow for some years. But before a woman can become a widow and get her pension and have her peace from men, she has to make it through her marriage, there's no getting around that, and after the age of thirty every woman was heading straight for spinsterhood if she hadn't found a man by then.

Grandma used to play canasta with her friends every Wednesday and she didn't like it when her friends said that people in the bakery and the pharmacy had been muttering about my mother, so they put their heads together and went through the handful of men who might be suitable, but they were all too old or were married or had been wounded in the war, having lost their marbles or limbs. All the same, Grandma obviously didn't want my mother to become an old spinster.

But the fact that it was Maria's son, that couldn't bode well, Grandma didn't need to be a fortune teller to work that one out, because the whole town knew what sort of life Maria was leading in Wallstrasse; she opened her door to anyone who still had most of his limbs intact.

I didn't understand everything Grandma and her friends said when they played cards on Wednesdays, but I heard that she couldn't stand my grandmother Maria because she lived in Wallstrasse and opened her door to anyone.

They said she'd opened her door to Herr Rose, the pub landlord, and the Gerickes from the fire brigade, both father and son, even someone from the choral society, it was said, that must be Woiwode, who wasn't quite all there because in the war his head had been split with the butt of a rifle and after the war they'd put a metal plate in his skull to keep the rest of his brain inside, but it was far too late.

When Grandma played canasta with her friends on Wednesdays there was usually nut cake or millefeuille. I would be given some too and listen to what they were saying. They certainly didn't believe that Maria had got her child from the Holy Ghost, but they didn't know whose it was as Maria wouldn't say, and because she'd fled from Belgium in the middle of the war and landed up here with the child, they could only surmise this or that, and while they drank coffee and later played canasta they pondered the fact that my grandmother had come from Ostend, and of course they knew that Ostend was a port and they knew what went on in ports: ships arrive from all over the world, including huge freighters from overseas. Even Chinese freighters put in there and as soon as the Chinese sailors set foot on dry land they, like every other sailor in this world, have precisely two things on their mind, nothing else. Chinese sailors have nothing on their mind apart from booze and women, Grandma and her friends were absolutely certain of that, and so the Chinese weren't any different from all other men, including Herr Rose the pub landlord, the Gerickes from the fire brigade and every single man in the choral society, whether they had a metal plate or not. And while I ate my child's portion of nut cake or my millefeuille, I learned from Grandma and her friends that it was probably a Chinese man who'd fished my father from the great black pool in Ostend when he was still a tadpole, and Grandma wasn't in the least surprised because she couldn't stand my father.

She couldn't stand him because when he came to visit he never helped her to hang the net curtains and heavy fabric curtains or to pick the pears from the tree even though he was young and strong, while she was old and not so strong any more, but it didn't occur to him to help her because after I was born he studied in East Berlin and students have other things on their minds than picking pears from the tree for their mother-in-law.

She called him Osch and even at that time my father couldn't stand it when people called him Osch. In fact everyone called him Osch apart from his own mother.

My grandmother Maria didn't see him very often because she lived in Wallstrasse and only rarely came to Grandma's house to visit her son and grandchild, and when she did come she never called my father Osch, but said, *du dommen jong*. That was Belgian and I thought that Belgian didn't sound so different from German, but apart from me nobody understood what my grandmother Maria said because she spoke Belgian rather than German. Most of the time she didn't speak at all, except for saying *du dommen jong* to her son, and to me she said *mijn meisje*, my girl.

She never stayed very long, because Grandma and she didn't have much to say to each other and because Grandma couldn't stand her son. She always brought me chocolate and left again soon afterwards, without giving me a slobbery kiss, but everyone knew that my father couldn't stand Grandma because she expected him to hang the curtains and pick pears from the tree, and also because she was stupid and cheated at cards.

He didn't especially object to her cheating at cards, it was just that she did it so stupidly that it was immediately obvious to everyone and it annoyed him, but I didn't find this out until later, when we were in the West, and he said, before a man gets involved with a woman he ought to take a look at her mother because she will be his mother-in-law, and in the case of Grandma he ought to have been warned.

If she could at least do it so it's not immediately obvious to everyone, he said, but she's too stupid even to cheat properly.

While he was still studying he tried whenever possible to avoid coming at the weekends, as he'd far rather stay in East Berlin, but because I'd been born and he was the father he had to come sometimes and go for walks in the Schlosspark with his wife and the pram.

They photographed each other pushing the pram because people would have talked if they hadn't gone for walks in the Schlosspark and taken pictures of each other. When she went for walks, my mother would peer into all the prams that came rolling past and as soon as she'd peered inside she would say, look, Osch, what a sweet baby, why don't we have a sweet baby like that with blonde hair, and look at its smile. My father would clench his fists and clamp his teeth together, and sometimes he said, don't keep calling me Osch, but I can't remember that because I was still in a pram and so I assume that everything was more or less fine until the day I met my father definitively, and from that day onwards I remember him clearly, even though he often wasn't there to begin with.

Meeting my father started with the hands and the rest followed afterwards and it was very creepy because it was dark and I wasn't able to talk yet. Afterwards they wanted me to forget it all, but I remember very clearly meeting my father, and I know I wished I could be back in the great black pool of eternity and swim in Neverland, because there it wasn't so cold or painful.

For that you don't need to be able to talk.

That evening someone had taken me from my cot and put me in Grandma's big bed in her dark room and I'd never been alone before in her dark room, where there was nothing but black all around me. To begin with I cried a little, because I was scared, then I cried a little more, because I was more scared, and in the end I started crying pretty loudly because there was nothing I could do about my fear and I was still too small to climb out of the big bed and leave the room or turn the light on, then finally I screamed as loudly as I could so someone would hear and fetch me from the darkness, and the door opened; a chink of light slanted into Grandma's bedroom from the hallway, but I couldn't see it clearly because I'd been put on my back with my head pointing towards the door and was still too small to sit up and turn my head, but now there was so much light coming from the hallway that I could see the huge paws coming at me from above through the darkness, these weren't human hands but paws, and they belonged to a monster standing on long hind legs with its arms stretched up in the air, and behind the huge paws a white face appeared, a long white face with black hair everywhere and a pair of sparkling discs, as big as the saucers in Grandma's lounge. Through the sparkles I couldn't see any eyes, only the two discs, and then those huge paws came down on me. One was clamped right across my face, which meant I couldn't breathe. Neither through my mouth nor through my nose. Summoning all my strength, I turned my head this way and that to try to get some air, I wiggled and struggled as much as I could and then for a moment I was able to draw breath and started to scream, but only for a moment, after which the paw squashed my face and pressed it hard against the pillow and I couldn't scream any more because my mouth was being forced shut, but I was just able to open it one last time and bite. The monster let out a terrifying howl and I was grabbed under my arms, hoisted into the air and shaken until my head hung loosely from my neck, flapping from side to side, and after that I was thrown against the wall.

Then the door closed again and it was dark. I wasn't lying in Grandma's bed any more, but on something hard and cold, and something was wrong. My head and everything on one side didn't feel right. It wasn't properly attached to the rest of my body any more, something had come loose and was stabbing me sharply and back to front. I could move my other side and my head was still attached to my neck, but it hung loosely. All five fingers were working on the hand I could still move, and I put my thumb in my mouth to stop myself from screaming, because screaming might make the door open again, so I closed my eyes and sucked my thumb, but this didn't calm me down, so I sucked more and harder and sucked for so long that I felt really dizzy and I could see nothing but gold and silver stars flashing and dancing in my closed eyes, and at some point the hard and cold in Grandma's dark room turned into the great black pool of eternity. It lapped softly at my feet to begin with, then got higher and higher, and finally it was all around me, it swallowed me, the stars vanished and underneath it stopped being cold and hard, my broken side wasn't there any more, nothing was stabbing me sharply and back to front, and everything was fine.

*

But I was still very small at the time, whereas now I was quite big and had already taken the bus by myself three times.

And that it's your bir-hirthday today.

I remembered Lisa's birthday, but that was two years ago when I was only five. Still, it was a very nice birthday.

Lisa was my best friend.

Actually she wasn't really my best friend because she lived in Sweden and I didn't know her in person, but Uncle Winkelmann had told me that it didn't matter whether you'd experienced a story personally or you'd read it or made it up, and that's how it was with Lisa. It didn't matter whether I knew her or had made her up or I'd read about her, and when I read Lisa's story of course I knew Lisa immediately, even though she lived in Sweden. By now she would be nine and I didn't know how she was, but when she was seven it was especially nice because she got hot chocolate and cake for breakfast and later that day her own room, her own room all to herself. It had been a surprise. Her parents had created everything in this room themselves: her father had put up wallpaper with little bunches of flowers and conjured up a chest of drawers, a round table and three chairs. He'd even built some bookshelves. And everything was painted white, and her mother had sewn curtains for the windows. But most beautiful of all were the colourful patchwork rugs with their red, yellow, green and black stripes, which she'd woven from her old scraps of material. And the whole time Lisa hadn't noticed a thing because her father was a carpenter and was always busy in his workshop making furniture for other people who couldn't do it themselves. So she thought nothing of it, and her mother was often sewing or sat at her loom, but it never occurred to Lisa that all of this might be for her and her new room. And shortly after her seventh birthday she got a kitten too.

When Lisa was seven we were still in the refugee camp and a room of my own was inconceivable, as was a kitten, but I was able to read.

I don't recall what it was like learning how to read. Mountains of books were piled on the table with the monkeys in the room where Auntie Eka, Uncle Grewatsch and Uncle Winkelmann lived. Some of the books had pictures of animals or the Alps. I liked the Alpine landscapes in particular: either they had no people in them at all, just mountains covered in snow, or mountains covered in snow with people on skis weaving through the snow. But most of the books had no pictures, just black chains of letters and, if you knew the letters, real stories emerged from them. There were as many different stories as you could wish for and you could pick them from the books and keep them like the apples that Auntie Eka, Uncle Winkelmann and I sometimes stole from the orchards and then Auntie Eka would put the pips in a small bowl on the windowsill to dry. When she'd gathered enough pips and they were dry she fetched a cotton reel and we'd string them all together until I had an apple-pip necklace.

On Lisa's birthday, when she was given her own room with the furniture, curtains and colourful patchwork rugs all made by her parents, and shortly after that a kitten, I was able to read.

If you can read you can perform magic and transport yourself to every country in the world, or change into an animal, or suddenly be in a different era from the one you're living in. You can travel around as you please, as if there were no fences or borders or walls to stop you, you don't get arrested, locked up or shot, and if you don't like the era you happen to be living in you can simply go back to another one, although I didn't especially want to go back to the era before I was born because I would have ended up bang in the middle of the war. But if you can read you can go everywhere, even into the future. Anyway, Uncle Winkelmann showed me a book with the story of a man who'd invented a time machine and who travelled into the future because he didn't particularly like the era he lived in. It was a big book which I wasn't yet able to read and it was far too big for anyone to read it to me, but when we had to say goodbye because their housing application had been approved, Uncle Winkelmann gave me his snow globe so I could go to Chengdu or Baghdad or Paris whenever I felt like it, and then he said he'd have something else for me when the time was ripe.

I couldn't believe it when he gave me the snow globe and I immediately wondered where to put it because it was so valuable and valuable treasures need to be well hidden, but I didn't know where, because I had nothing of my own in which I could hide something.

Then I thought about what Uncle Winkelmann had just said.

When will the time be ripe? I asked, and he said, when it is we'll know.

Ever since Lisa's birthday I knew, at any rate, what paradise was, and I resolved never to forget it, but now, on my seventh birthday, I found it difficult not to forget paradise because in order to remember it I urgently needed someone I could talk to about it. Lisa. Or Auntie Eka, Uncle Grewatsch, Uncle Winkelmann.

We weren't in paradise but in the Promised Land, and though I tried my best I still couldn't understand how things could have turned out this way.

> *We love you and give you*
> *things to eat, drink and play with.*

I didn't have to kid myself about the love part, as it was clear from the beginning that nothing would come of it.

As far as the food was concerned, the disaster began in the refugee camp. When we were still in the East, Grandma cooked us proper lunches and baked cakes and in the evenings we'd have plates of cold cuts and black pudding. My mother didn't have a hand in any of it, and I thought they ought to have taken this into account before we fled from the East, and the more I thought about it the less clear it became why they'd fled in the first place, because we'd been better off at Grandma's, even without all the promises. There were lots of rooms in her house, more at any rate than in our flat on the estate, and also the lounge with the veranda. I liked the veranda. In one corner there was always a large vase full of bulrushes, and in summer the bulrushes were taken out and replaced with sunflowers that would shine in the afternoons when Grandma and her friends ate cake and played canasta and Grandma always won because she cheated. But by the time she'd won the sun had moved across the veranda and just before it vanished the sunflowers in the vase would begin to shine like crazy, and they'd continue to shine for a while longer once the sun had disappeared and it was time for supper and the plates of cold cuts arrived on the table.

I'd never thought about food until we were in the refugee camp and Auntie Eka sometimes said, my girl, have you had anything to eat at all?

I think so, I'd usually reply.

She said, what does I think so mean? but I really couldn't remember because in the refugee camp we had either dumplings with white sauce or milk soup, which my mother would cook in the communal kitchen because she'd never cooked anything before and so didn't know how to cook, and from wartime she knew that there was starch in flour so she took the flour, stirred it with water, and on the ration card we were given in the refugee camp it also said 'fat'. My mother stirred the fat into the starch as well until everything congealed and she rolled it into dumplings, which she put into hot water. While the dumplings were cooking she made the sauce. She prepared it in a similar way to how she made milk soup, except for this one she put the fat into a pan and waited until it hissed before pouring the flour in and stirring until everything was brown and finally she poured in water. For milk soup she used the milk we got from the camp management because I was a child and children had a milk allowance. She preferred making dumplings to milk soup because there were two risky moments in the milk soup recipe that she was anxious about. Whereas for the white sauce there was only one risky moment. The fat could turn black rather than brown when my mother added the starch and then the sauce or the soup would taste burnt later. When she made the soup the milk would usually boil over at the end, which meant the entire communal kitchen would smell burnt. Nothing bad would happen to the milk soup, but the boiled-over milk smelled disgusting and the Romanian and Bulgarian women, who were also in the camp and cooked with us in the communal kitchen, would fling open the windows and laugh. My mother hated it when they laughed. She hated it too that we'd been scheduled to cook with them because the camp management had made a mistake when dividing everyone up and we weren't scheduled to cook until half past one, when all the Germans had finished, but by twelve o'clock there wasn't a single free hob in the kitchen so my mother couldn't do anything about it.

If I was lucky the dumplings with white sauce and the milk soup smelled and tasted of nothing, and as soon as I'd gobbled everything up and waited to see whether it stayed down I forgot that I'd eaten at all.

It smelled good in the communal kitchen, not on account of the food my mother cooked but because of the Romanian and Bulgarian women. As they cooked they would talk and laugh and taste from each other's pots and pans. Their children were always there, quite a lot of them, and they would taste from the pots and pans too.

The chattering in the kitchen was like a jolly melody and the food smelled of spices I didn't know. It reminded me of the delicacies from Chengdu or Paris and the hustle and bustle of the market in Baghdad, which Uncle Winkelmann always talked about when I shook his snow globe on one of the cities in the world or when he read to me from one of his books.

That was what I loved about the refugee camp. Because Uncle Winkelmann told me everything and read to me from his books, I could remember at once all the unfamiliar spices in the communal kitchen even though I didn't know them and had never smelled them before, but Uncle Winkelmann and the stories of letters threaded together into his books talked about these spices in such detail that I could smell them and each time I was desperate to try a spoonful.

It wasn't like Grandma's roast rabbit or veal kidney chops, even though I could smell the aromas of her kitchen too. The longer we were in the refugee camp the more I missed those familiar aromas.

The communal kitchen smelled different. It smelled unfamiliar, exciting and enticing, and I would have loved to try the food. Sometimes one of the women offered me her wooden spoon so I could have a taste, but my mother would grab me firmly by the arm and pull me over to the dumplings or milk soup that she had cooked herself.

When we were back in our room she would say that we didn't want to eat any of the Romanian or Bulgarian women's food because they weren't German, but came from Romania and Bulgaria and the way they reeked of garlic they were probably gypsies.

Sometimes when I went over to see them, Auntie Eka had put some leftover lentil or potato soup from lunch in a little pot on the windowsill where she also put the apples that we stole and didn't eat straight away, and then Uncle Grewatsch would take me to the communal kitchen, which was pretty empty and quiet in the afternoons, though the unfamiliar smell still lingered in the air, and we would warm up a bowl of soup. Lentil soup and potato soup were my favourite meals and later I was allowed to stand on a stool and wash up the pot and my bowl myself, while Uncle Grewatsch dried.

*

When we were all still living in the East there was nothing special about the food. There wasn't even anything special about nut cake or raspberry roulade, because Grandma made them every Wednesday when her friends came, sometimes a quark and cream tart or millefeuille too. All morning her kitchen would smell of baking and on Saturdays she would bake again, because it was the weekend and maybe one of her sons, or even both of them, would come from East Berlin, and I thought this was normal and how life was. On Sundays she cooked rabbit, veal kidney chops with chanterelles, sauerkraut with smoked gammon and many other Sunday dishes, and I liked the smell of roasting meat at least as much as that of cakes, if not more, and every evening she would prepare platters of cold cuts or slices of bread with rillettes or black pudding, and of course I never thought about this when I was young because that's how it was.

By now I'd found out that my mother didn't care what she ate.

My father and I, on the other hand, did care, but during the war my mother had been in the Labour Service. In the Labour Service everyone had always eaten together and my mother didn't care what there was to eat because under the Nazis it wasn't important, at least not for those in the Labour Service, and because she was engaged and after the war she'd marry her landowner fiancé, although they of course did care, the landowners obviously had a cook who was at least as good as Grandma. The thing

in the Labour Service was that a leader of the League of
German Girls would sit with the others at the table, and
she really didn't care because she was an A1 Nazi from
the League of German Girls and for her the important
thing was that it was over quickly, so she would wolf it
down, and hardly had the others picked up their knives
and forks and begun than she'd already got her food down
her, and when she'd got her food down her this signalled
that the meal was over for everyone at the table, finished.
That's why my mother ate so quickly and why she didn't
care what she ate.

It was only ever different at the Schwanen.

The Schwanen belonged to our gymnastics association and sometimes my father would go there with his
colleagues, and when the red factory workers went to
the Schwanen they had their fixed routine, which hadn't
changed since the war. Either they booked the bowling
alley, and if they went bowling it was usually only the
men who went, occasionally their fiancées or new brides,
so long as there weren't any children the wives had to
look after at home, and they didn't have anything to eat
because they had a liquid supper when they went bowling
and came home very late and very drunk. Or they went
to the restaurant, which they always did if someone had
an anniversary or a big birthday, something like that,
and then all the wives and children would normally come
along too. At the school where my mother worked her
colleagues didn't go to the Schwanen, or anywhere else,

but there were teacher awaydays, parents' evenings and Christmas parties. On those occasions my father and I would stay at home on our own, my father would whistle his favourite aria from Mozart's *Don Giovanni*, 'Là ci darem la mano', and after he'd get comfy with me on the couch, pour himself a submarine and then another, and say that I was his little mouse and princess and he wasn't the type of man to waste his youth, but sometimes his colleagues at the red factory went to the Schwanen.

The Schwanen's speciality was different types of schnitzel. Apart from schnitzel there was all manner of stuff on the menu, beef and onion stew, herring salad or Serbian bean soup, and for children and those who weren't particularly hungry there was bread with liver pâté.

Everyone always spent a while deliberating over whether they should have the hunter's schnitzel, Puszta schnitzel, cream schnitzel or in fact the Wiener schnitzel. They even had gypsy's schnitzel on the menu, though I thought we wouldn't eat any gypsy food because we were Germans, or at least my mother was, albeit not proper West Germans. My father was neither one thing nor the other and children take after their father because it's the father who fishes you out of the pond, so I wasn't German either, but being Belgian was similar to being German, at any rate it wasn't gypsy.

Someone would occasionally order the gypsy's schnitzel and it was no big deal. Clearly everyone at the Schwanen thought it perfectly normal to eat a gypsy's schnitzel, and it struck me that nobody can ever work out what's right and what's not if people lie to them all the time.

When we were at the Schwanen my father usually ordered the beef and onion stew, while my mother would spend a long time pondering what to have, what she fancied just at that moment, then she'd order something, and it didn't matter what she ordered because the moment the food arrived she'd realize that she'd made the wrong choice.

She always realized as soon as the food was put in front of her.

How could I have been so silly? she said, pushing her plate away a few centimetres because she'd suddenly realized that she couldn't possibly eat a cream schnitzel now, not for all the world, and that the person sitting next to her had been much cannier and had made a far better choice from the menu.

You were spot on, she said. Mushroom sauce is exactly what I fancy right now, I bet it's nice and tart, not heavy like what I ordered.

She looked at her plate in disgust.

Even the sight of it makes my stomach turn, she said to the person sitting next to her, usually a man because the couples were always mixed up, a man beside a woman he wasn't married to, and then the woman's child or children and so on.

My father didn't notice any of this. He was sitting a bit further down the table so he couldn't hear anything, but ate his beef and onion stew and talked to the woman next to him about the Salzkammergut or what was on television and whether or not her children were allowed to watch Francis Durbridge films yet. Every parent always said that their children weren't allowed to watch Francis Durbridge films because they were gory and not for children, but that couldn't be right because there were plenty of children who'd seen the films and who talked about them all day long in the playground and on the estate.

Anyway, my father didn't have to say anything about my mother having chosen the cream schnitzel she didn't fancy any more, but the person next to her with his mushroom sauce did have to say something because my mother had spoken to him directly and was envious of his mushroom sauce.

Usually he'd say, bad luck, it happens.

Or he'd say, that's happened to me before. When you look at the menu you imagine something else and only when they serve it up do you realize that it wasn't what you wanted.

Once my mother sat beside Our-Uwe, who was very nice. As soon as my mother found even the sight of her cream schnitzel too heavy he said it wasn't a problem, he didn't mind what he had here because everything at the Schwanen tasted pretty much the same, it all tasted of Maggi, and then he offered to swap dishes with my mother as neither had started eating and the schnitzels hadn't even been cut up.

My mother wouldn't accept the hunter's schnitzel, however, even though she said, you're a real gentleman, Herr Doktor; she wouldn't accept it.

Things went on like this for a while until the schnitzels had gone cold and Our-Uwe was really keen to eat one of them, no matter whether it was with cream or mushrooms.

Thank you very much, Herr Doktor, she said, it's very kind of you, but I'm the one who ordered the cream schnitzel so now I've got to face the music and suffer the consequences, serves me right.

Our-Uwe said that a cream schnitzel wasn't exactly a lifelong burden you had to shoulder, and he offered to swap again, but it always ended up with my mother insisting she finish up her plate herself. She pulled it towards her and sighed. Then she'd usually glance longingly at my bread and liver pâté and say, you chose well. Bread and liver pâté would have been perfectly fine. But she didn't ask me to swap with her and I didn't say that I'd made a good or bad choice, or any choice at all, because children weren't given a menu, they were just given bread and liver pâté, and I wouldn't have swapped with my mother because I always looked forward to going to the Schwanen as the bread and liver pâté reminded me of the cold cuts and rillettes and black pudding in the East, and there was also a gherkin cut into a tiny fan shape which almost tasted like the salted gherkins at Grandma's.

On the way home my mother always said that the cream schnitzel was too heavy and salty, and if my father said nothing but put his hands in his coat pockets she'd add that she liked it nonetheless.

My father continued to say nothing and I said nothing either, because I hoped that the matter was now closed, but it always rumbled on a little further.

After all, the schnitzel did cost six marks eighty, my mother said. I really think it ought to taste nice. At that price.

And if we hadn't yet got to the front steps of our building she would say, what we do for our career. We'll even eat an over-salted schnitzel for six marks eighty.

And can you remember, Osch, how many beers you had? she said, before we went up the steps. Was it three or four?

And things were exactly the same when I was born, or pretty similar, even if the birthday song made it sound very different, but my parents weren't happy when I was born, or at least my mother always said it was a disaster, and now I was seven and so I'd had some time to find out what it was like.

Until I came into play everything was pretty much OK, but then my father had to turn twenty-one and after that they had to get married because otherwise my father would have had no official authorization for having given my mother a baby, and then everyone would have said that like Maria she opened her door to anyone, and that was even worse than being an old spinster.

The wedding took place in late winter and at that time of year it wasn't easy to rustle up the green salad with its creamy dressing that my mother had to eat every day so that the little frog in her belly would turn into a human being. In Grandma's garden the salad didn't start growing until spring, when everything else started growing too, the strawberries, the borage and the chives for the salad, and it was always a bit of a mystery to me how my mother managed to come by green salad in February; I think the salad was another lie. It was ice-cold at their wedding and on the way to the register office the bunch of lavender, which she was holding in front of her tummy to prevent the photos from showing that it was pretty big already, froze.

Afterwards the tummy got bigger and bigger and by the beginning of summer the time had come.

But no, my mother said, when she talked about my birth, little madam didn't care about punctuality, you took your time and put yourself on hold.

My mother was punctuality personified and couldn't stand it when people weren't punctual.

After she'd pleaded with me for four weeks and the pond water in her tummy was no longer see-through and colourless, but was gradually turning cloudy and green, the little madam finally heard the pleas and deigned to enter this world, at the very time when the doctor had gone on holiday and there was only the caretaker in the hospital to help my mother. The doctor was on Rügen and the caretaker had no idea how to help a woman give birth and so the story almost went badly wrong.

It tore me into two, right down the middle, my mother said, those bloody pains.

Or she'd say, I just wanted to die. Leave that vale of tears.

Sometimes she also said, I cursed God, but I didn't believe her because, like everyone from our part of eastern Germany, she was Prussian and Protestant. If the Protestants believe in anything at all they believe only in what they can see and of course they can't see God. Nobody can see him because he hovers above the Holy Ghost, in who they don't believe either because they can't see him, and so they just pretend, which basically means it was irrelevant who my mother cursed, and I fear she cursed me, because it was my fault that she had to start eating this disgusting green salad with creamy dressing, and that she was torn into two, right down the middle, and that she just wanted to leave that vale of tears and would rather have died than give birth to me. Anyway, I wasn't blue when I was born, but that was the only positive thing. The umbilical cord didn't wrap itself once around my neck and an hour after I was born there were green beans to eat in the hospital. This partly distracted my mother from the distress she'd gone through. It was only when my father arrived at the hospital to take a look at the child that she remembered it was a hideous spawn from the outset, something she'd almost forgotten while eating the green beans, but when my father came she remembered, because of course my father could see at once that he'd had bad luck when fishing the tadpole from the great black pool of eternity, containing billions and billions of other tadpoles, each one prettier than the next, any of which he could have fished out, and which would have turned into beaming little boys with blond hair, but he had to catch the very tadpole which would turn into the most ugly human being of all time, a wet, wrinkled something with a bright-red face and covered all over with black hair.

I got a real fright, my mother said when she talked about it.

> We're so happy you were born
> and that it's your bir-hirthday today,

she now sang for the third time, but even at the third time my father didn't join in. It's actually a very short song and I'm certain my mother would have liked to sing a longer one afterwards because she was in a festive mood seeing as it was my birthday, but after watching her for a while my father clenched his fists, and when he clenched his fists the four knuckles between his fingers and the back of his hand first went a much lighter colour, then after a while, when the blood had drained from them, turned white. I couldn't see the knuckle on the thumb, but I suspect it turned white too, and finally the jaw muscles in his face started to move, and they moved in a way that made his teeth grind. The teeth grinding didn't go with the singing at all so my mother skipped the longer song and instead repeated the shorter one a few times, and each time it sounded ridiculous when she sang 'bir-hirthday'. Ridiculous and sad. Almost as if she were crying, and there were two more lines after that:

> *We love you and give you*
> *things to eat, drink and play with.*

I had to watch out that I didn't start crying myself when I thought of the nut cake and the biscuit roll in Grandma's lounge, of the aromas in her kitchen and the kitten I'd been wanting ever since my fifth birthday because kittens like nothing better than to play. You can tie a scrap of paper to some string and run around with it and kittens run after you and leap about to catch the paper, and they look so funny that you fall about laughing, but just before I felt sorry for myself because I didn't have a kitten I imagined again how disappointed my parents must have been when the translucent tadpole my father had fished out of the black pool of eternity even before he was of age turned out to be such an ugly human being. And a girl to boot. And so I felt more sorry for them than for myself.

Anyway, on my seventh birthday I resolved that I'd get a kitten at some point and as soon as I'd got the kitten I'd know it was a belated seventh birthday present, and I already knew now how lucky I'd be.

My parents, on the other hand, probably wouldn't be rid of the failure that had come into their life seven years ago any time soon, because they hadn't managed to be rid of it yet, even though they'd gone to some effort, but without success, and I'd tried myself, again and again, and now it was summer. If I hadn't succeeded in winter it certainly wouldn't work now, because I could stand by the open window taking deep breaths as often as I liked, and the air outside was warm, unlike the winter air that was icy and despite this had failed to give me pneumonia, even when I lasted almost an hour by the open window to see how many stars there were in the night and how many tadpoles in the great black pool, and if I'd got pneumonia by the open window it would have all been over, I'd have gone back to the pool because that's what happens to you when you get pneumonia or you're shot or die some other way. But I didn't get pneumonia. Not even a cold.

After she'd finished singing the birthday song, my mother told me about my birth, and when she was finished with that she said, I loved you nonetheless.

I thought that when she said 'nonetheless' she always meant the opposite, just like with the cream schnitzel at the Schwanen. When she said that she liked the cream schnitzel nonetheless, it was worse than if she'd said straight out that she hadn't liked it.

I wouldn't have thought it so bad if she'd said, actually I wanted a different child, not one with black hair, I'd have preferred a little blond boy, but you never know with these things and I was just unlucky.

We could have lived with that, I thought.

Rather no love than nonetheless, I thought, because basically you couldn't do anything with nonetheless.

When the song was over it was time for the birthday cake. On birthdays there was always hedgehog slice. I actually liked hedgehog slice; it just made you very thirsty.

In the birthday song it says, we give you things to eat, drink and play with, so I thought I might be able to have something to drink with the cake. Not necessarily hot chocolate or warm milk, just something to quench the thirst you get from hedgehog slice.

When I'd eaten a piece I said tentatively, I'm really very thirsty after the hedgehog slice.

My mother said, but you had something to drink this morning.

I couldn't remember whether I'd had anything to drink that morning, but I said, hedgehog slice makes you thirsty.

My father didn't like hedgehog slice, he hadn't touched it and he'd put his glass of Coca-Cola on the coffee table beside him. You never knew whether my father was thirsty or not, because he always had a glass to hand when he came home from work, and he drank either Coca-Cola, sometimes with something in it and sometimes without, or beer. He only drank submarines if my mother had a parents' evening or a Christmas party.

My mother didn't drink anything because she was never thirsty. In the mornings she'd have a cup of coffee and in the evenings a cup of tea, but never anything in between, and when she drank her tea in the evenings she said that she wasn't at all thirsty.

I don't know how you do it, Osch, she said when my father refilled his beer glass, and usually she'd add, I just drink because it's sensible. I really have to force myself to.

I was very often thirsty between the morning and the evening, but if I said I was thirsty my mother would say, but you had something to drink this morning.

If, despite this, I was still thirsty, she'd say, surely you're not diabetic.

Then she told me what it was like to be diabetic; slowly and gradually the disease dissolved all your internal organs and you had to get an injection every day.

Finally she'd tell me that it wasn't nice, and after that, although I was still thirsty, I preferred not to say any more that I was because I didn't under any circumstances want to be diabetic and get an injection every day, even though I wasn't sure whether to believe her or not and whether diabetes and the dissolving internal organs were like the cherry tree that grew out of your throat.

But you could never know.

Basically you could never know anything.

And in the end I don't even know what happened after that on my birthday, because you couldn't know for sure, not in our flat.

I'd got a mass of presents. Grandma had embroidered handkerchiefs for me and wrapped them beautifully. My other grandmother had sent me a manicure set with a file and lots of little sticks for cleaning your nails. The manicure set smelled nice, and when I said it smelled nice my father said, plastic and elastic.

From one of my uncles I got a pink, square-shaped single because he thought we had a record player, but we didn't have one because my mother couldn't stand the music my father liked to listen to, and in order to listen to music we would go to the Centenary Hall with its huge domed roof that looked like a turtle's shell, because everyone who wanted to climb the ladder at the red factory went there, they all dressed up smartly, my mother put on her georgette gown and then we'd listen to music until the interval. My mother used to cry because she was filled with longing for her dead father and her brothers, and during the interval everyone would say, *Guten Tag, Herr Doktor*, and drink Sekt. If my father was going off to get Sekt, my mother would say, not for me, Osch, you know Sekt doesn't agree with me. Then she looked to see whether Our-Uwe was nearby and usually he and his wife were nearby, drinking Sekt too, and then my mother would say, I'll tell you now, Herr Doktor, Sekt doesn't agree with me, it always makes me tipsy, and after the interval the music would continue.

My other uncle had forgotten my birthday, and my mother said that he was so distracted at the moment because his wife had given birth to another child.

It was the uncle whose ear had been bitten off by a horse during the war and this was already his fifth child.

My mother said, I hope the stable's full now, I don't know what they're thinking.

My father said there wasn't necessarily much thought involved.

Then they gave me the package from Auntie Eka, Uncle Winkelmann and Uncle Grewatsch. Inside was a big, old book I knew, and when I saw it my heart missed a beat.

The Time Machine. On the book was a postcard with birthday wishes from all three of them. Each of them had signed it individually and at the bottom Uncle Winkelmann had added in block capitals: We think that now, on your birthday, the time is ripe.

I at once recalled our conversation in the refugee camp, even though I still didn't know what a ripe time was, and after that everything happened very quickly, because this time Wolfi the doll's head came off on my birthday and I said that I was too big to be playing with dollies anyway.

Almost nothing occurred as a result, except for my father lighting a cigarette and saying very softly, I'm warning you, little madam.

I thought that everything was different on birthdays, so I didn't take the warning seriously.

Next I unwrapped the big present that had been sitting all this time in the birch-wood wall unit in my parents' bedroom.

There was no postcard inside this one, because my parents were here, standing in the lounge and waiting to see the delight on my face.

Forewarned, I unwrapped the present. It was a huge globe and I started showing my delight, because my parents were watching me and because you could see the whole world on the globe and travel with your finger to all the countries and cities where Uncle Winkelmann had been on his journeys across the oceans and where I'd go that very same afternoon, to Chengdu or Baghdad or Paris. The whole world.

The globe was on a stand and you could spin it. On the front of the stand, at the bottom, there was a switch and behind it a lead with a plug. If you plugged it in and pressed the switch the globe started to glow from the inside.

My father showed me how it worked. The globe glowed faintly, but not much at the moment because it was summer and nowhere near dark yet, which was why you could barely see it and I'd soon forgotten that it glowed and that the lead was attached to a plug. In fact I'd completely forgotten that there was a lead at all, and I spun the globe as if it didn't have a lead, and then it happened, and of course I didn't do it deliberately, I just tripped over the lead and fell, the globe crashed to the floor, it didn't glow any more and on the underside, where South America was, the sphere was dented.

I warned you, my father said, and then I knew that this time my birthday would turn out different from previous ones.

In the refugee camp I'd sometimes been able to slip out of the door, but on the new estate that wasn't possible.

All the same I'd usually slip off somewhere when it all kicked off.

Usually it would kick off gently, with my father saying things like, I warned you. Sometimes he'd also ask, are you trying to take me for an idiot?

He couldn't bear it if someone was an idiot, and he really couldn't bear it if someone tried to take him for an idiot, but obviously I wasn't trying to take him for an idiot because I didn't exactly know what that meant and how you did it.

Occasionally he'd say, don't you do that to me, even though I'd done nothing to him or even intended to do anything, it was just a phrase that told me I ought to get to safety now because it was about to kick off.

There were a lot of phrases that told me this.

So, my father said, you want something else to happen today, do you?

No, I said. Please don't. I don't want anything else to happen today.

But he'd decided that I did want something else to happen today, and in a flash I'd slip behind the couch before that something else could happen, or under a chair, or, like the seventh little goat in the fairy tale, I'd slip into the case of the large teak grandfather clock that my father had to reset to eight o'clock every evening when the news was on because it lost seven minutes each day. It didn't show the weather correctly either.

It was an ugly clock with a brass pendulum that always swung back and forth.

As soon as I'd got myself to safety I could follow that something else happening from my hiding place, and watch how it always kicked off gently, making you think that this time it might not be so bad, but of course it never stopped at my father saying, I'm not having that, you're not doing that to me.

Inside the teak casing I could always hear the reassuring ticking of the ugly clock. Obviously it's not nice for the seventh little goat to have to see and hear the wolf eating up his six brothers and sisters, be forced to listen to the screams of those poor creatures outside. It's a while before they're all finally dead and torn to pieces and gobbled up.

Although the poor creature I had to look at wasn't gobbled up, it was badly treated all the same.

I listened to it whimpering.

It said, please, not on the face.

Then it put its hands over its mouth, because it didn't want to be hit on the mouth, and then I heard the man's voice saying, kindly take your hands away from your face, but it didn't take its hands away and used them both to cover its mouth.

It looked like one of the three monkeys on the table at Auntie Eka, Uncle Grewatsch and Uncle Winkelmann's. One is covering its eyes, one its ears and the third one its mouth, but I didn't have time to think about the monkeys, because there was always more to come and it wasn't so gentle, and it always ended with the creature lying doubled up on the floor, no longer covering its mouth, but its entire head so the clog couldn't kick the head, or because the clog had already kicked the head; I couldn't see exactly, from the clock case.

The ticking of the large brass pendulum always made me tired and at some point the great black pool of eternity came, lapping softly at my feet, then got higher and higher and eventually it was all around and swallowed me.

Only this time I hadn't been taking care because I thought it was different on birthdays.

I'd been warned, but I hadn't taken the warning seriously and hadn't been able to slip into the clock case, behind the couch or anywhere else in time and get myself to safety.

At some point it was dark, even though it was summer and light till late. I was lying in bed in my dark room.

My face was burning; inside me everything felt spiky and prickly.

It could be my bones, I thought, because Isolde Ickstadt had said there was something wrong with my bones, and I felt sick. I opened the window and threw up, but I still felt sick and as if I were about to black out. But I didn't black out. From outside the moon shone into my room and I could just about see that there were endless stars in the sky.

On my bedspread were Wolfi the doll and his head, and all the other presents, six embroidered handkerchiefs, the manicure set, the square single and the book.

The Time Machine.

I read the postcard again, especially the PS at the bottom.

The ripe time.

The broken globe stood at the foot of the bed. I looked under the pillow because I was suddenly scared that my snow globe might no longer be there, but it was.

And then I had an idea.

It was a very good idea, I realized this at once, but only much later did I understand how good the idea was.

The Time Machine was on my pillow and all of a sudden it was crystal clear to me that the time was ripe now.

Auntie Eka, Uncle Winkelmann and Uncle Grewatsch had known it, and I knew it too. The time was ripe now and I ought to grasp it, because it wouldn't come my way again.

It was now and I would grasp it because it was ripe.

It was a decision.

I reached for Uncle Winkelmann's snow globe and shut my eyes so tightly that there was a flashing and twinkling behind the lids, then I opened them again because I wanted to see what this ripe time looked like, and I assumed that when I opened them I'd see all around me the dark room in which I'd awoken, but my room wasn't dark any more; it was brightly lit. Light flickered through the room, all around me a wild blaze of light, it didn't stop flashing and twinkling and, with the snow globe in my hand, I got out of bed, the whole room flashing and twinkling, and on the floor at the foot of my bed lay the globe that couldn't glow any more because I'd broken it. I hadn't done it on purpose, but it would have been better if I had broken my birthday present on purpose; it was flashing like crazy around the globe. I reached through the flashes and started to spin it. Carefully and delicately at first, but then faster and faster.

I sat on the bed, spinning the globe wildly with my right hand, then started to shake the snow globe with my left, the snow in the globe fell on some city in the world, on Chengdu, on Baghdad or on Paris, I didn't know. Uncle Winkelmann would have known, but he wasn't there.

Nobody was there apart from me.

The globe spun faster and faster, and as it spun like crazy the city in my snow globe changed, houses were pulled down, new houses rose inside the snow globe, huge skyscrapers with twinkling glass roofs, trees disappeared, the streets grew wider and wider, there were no longer just two or three cars driving around the streets but lots…the globe spun so quickly that it became hot in the room and it hissed, me spinning with the globe. Uncle Winkelmann had told me about Baron Münchhausen, who had ridden against the Turks on a cannonball – the snow globe spun, the sky spun, the universe spun, then we took off, sparks flying everywhere.

All of this happened simply because I wanted it to, and I wanted to go further and further away: the window in my bedroom shattered because the globe was picking up speed, my room was too small for such speed, the changes in my snow globe picked up speed too, everything became electric and blinked, I kept shaking, but no matter how much snow fell it couldn't cover the world, it didn't even look white, but grey, like ashes. There was a bang as the globe shot with me and my snow globe through the shattered window and into the black sky, into the night, into the blackness.

This was what the speed of light must be like, and as we flew through the black at the speed of light there was nothing in my head save for a single thought: I want to meet myself, I want to meet myself. In forty years to the day. It was a brilliant thought down to the smallest detail, for in forty years' time I'd be roughly as old and as clever as Uncle Winkelmann, who in any case was older than my parents and must be pushing fifty, at least that's what my mother said when she told me in the refugee camp how the three of them were carrying on, and now the time was ripe. Auntie Eka, Uncle Grewatsch and Uncle Winkelmann had known it and I knew it too: in forty years to the day.

I'd done it. At the ripe time I'd shot myself into the future and made a crucial appointment.

I'd meet myself on 5 July 2003. The year 2003 was in the next century, which slightly frightened me, and the thought that I'd just shot myself into the next century made me feel a bit queasy and weak, and I can't remember what happened after that. At any rate, I was out of it for quite a while, and when I awoke I knew that it had been the result of the huge exertion of my superhuman ride on the globe and I knew too that I'd done it.

My hand was clutching the snow globe; some city in the world was waiting for the snow to fall, but I was too feeble to lift my hand and shake the globe.

Isolde Ickstadt was sitting by my bed. Her updo had survived the journey perfectly, in her bright-red cabriolet with its open top; it hadn't collapsed, nor was it even dishevelled, but perhaps I wasn't able to see properly because I could only look at everything from a distance through a thick fog.

The doctor said something about cardiac cycle, but of course it had nothing to do with any cycle. I'd just broken the cycle.

I waited quite a while and nothing happened.

I'd hoped that something would have changed.

At any rate, I had travelled to the year 2003, if only for a brief moment, to say that I needed someone to talk to. That I needed someone to help me.

Isolde Ickstadt had got up and left the room with my mother.

Nobody was there. I'll probably be long dead in forty years' time anyway, I thought.

Then I heard the voice and knew at once that it was my own voice, even though it sounded much deeper.

It said, good God.

I said nothing so I could hear whether the voice was going to say anything else.

It's time to get cracking, it said.

After that it was quiet for a long while, before I heard a noise like someone grinding their teeth.

Let's get on with it, then, the voice said eventually, and I was keen to see what we would be getting on with.

To begin with, however, we didn't intend anything exciting, because I liked going to Herr Grashopp's 1B class, even though I could already read and found it boring to just draw colourful snails in my exercise book all the time rather than chains of letters. At break all the children got milk, even though the war had been over for years and we'd long been living in the Promised Land, where everyone had enough to eat and drink, but nobody fully trusted the peace. So, just in case, there was still milk and cod-liver oil at school. At break the children talked of war and said that the Russians might be coming soon and we'd have to get everything to safety, roll up the carpets and hide the women and girls, because the Russians were particularly keen on carpets and women and girls, the blonder the better – they'd even take the old ones if they had to – and coming from the East I was of course suspect, because the East was swarming with Russians, who were just beyond the border, waiting to get their hands on the West German carpets and women.

*

We liked Herr Grashopp's class, even though the way he combed his few strands of hair across his bald head from the left ear to the right looked ridiculous. At break there was milk and it was while we were all drinking our milk that it happened for the first time.

We were all frightened of Harald because he bashed everyone up. I stayed well clear of him because he particularly liked to have a go at the little ones.

Tassilo was a little one. Once Harald kept on calling him a wop until he got so mad that he punched him in the stomach. It looked funny because he struck out with both fists a few times and Harald just stood there, watching with amusement, and only then did it really kick off.

Suddenly Harald pretended he had to hold his stomach and he groaned something.

That hit the spot, he said.

But then he laughed again and asked, do you want something, little boy?

Tassilo didn't want anything. He just wanted not to be called a wop, but Harald had it in for him and said he was the son of an Eyetie whore, which made Tassilo even angrier than being called a wop. He looked around to see whether Herr Grashopp or Frau Helminger were in the playground, because they took turns to do duty, but neither was anywhere to be seen.

Grabbing Tassilo by the shoulder, Harald twisted his arm and put him in a headlock. Then he said, you're going to start snivelling, aren't you, little boy, cos no one can help you now and I'm going to make mincemeat of you.

And don't bother trying to call bald old Grasshopper, he can't help you either cos they castrated him in the war.

Shot to the head, then castrated, he said, circling his palm in front of his face a few times, and if you really want to know, he's gaga anyway.

And at that moment I heard my voice.

It sounded much deeper than my child's voice, but it was mine and it said, shot to the head and gaga? What rubbish! Tell them what it was like.

I had no idea what the voice meant, because I didn't know what that was like or what on earth Harald was talking about.

Then I took a deep breath and said to Harald, you haven't got a clue.

Harald turned to me and said, do you want something?

I said, Herr Grashopp was at Monte Cassino.

Monte Cassino only came to mind because it had to do with the war and because Uncle Winkelmann had said time and again that he'd fled from Monte Cassino and defected to the Poles, and that's why he'd ended up in Russia.

Sometimes words come to mind just like that, without you being able to say why.

What do you know about Monte Cassino? Harald asked scornfully.

All the boys thought that girls knew nothing about the war because they hadn't been at the front, but I didn't think that Harald had been at the front either and so he didn't know any more about the war than I did.

After he released Tassilo from the headlock, I told them both how Herr Grashopp had been with the paratroopers, just a few hundred metres from the Catholic monastery, obviously the monastery was on a mountain, or at least I believed that monasteries were on mountains, and inside the monastery were lots of world-famous priceless treasures, which Herr Grashopp was certain would be destroyed in the battle for the monastery, and I kept talking about the priceless treasures and the bombers and fighter aircraft and tanks and monks, and finally I said that Herr Grashopp was a hero because he tried to save the monastery's treasures, and when he got into the cellar he caught a few comrades from his brigade drinking the Communion wine and quite casually smashing all the monastery treasures they could get their hands on, even though the monks kept begging them to leave these things alone.

But in vain, I said. These men were totally screwed up by the war and quite drunk to boot. They stole half the treasures and smashed the rest to smithereens.

Uncle Winkelmann had said that all soldiers had been screwed up by the war, but 'screwed up' was not exactly something little girls said.

Here I paused in the hope that Harald was Catholic, because otherwise he'd definitely be on the soldiers' side.

In addition to Tassilo and Harald there were now a few more children around me, quite a lot in fact, and Harald said, you certainly seem to know a lot about it.

What happened to Herr Grashopp after that? someone from the third form asked, and I told them how Herr Grashopp was injured by one of his own comrades, no idea how, either the butt of a rifle had smashed his skull or a bullet had been fired by accident and then bang, I said. It doesn't matter whether it was deliberate or not, I said, in any case the monks took him to safety and looked after him in their vaults until the bloodbath was over and he could go to hospital, and he was still half dead and since then he's had the metal plate inside his head. You all know that.

I pointed to the crown of my head.

Everybody was completely silent.

His life was on a knife-edge, I said, and someone said, God.

They operated on him for fourteen hours, I said with a sigh.

That's why he's got the funny haircut, I said, concluding my story, and thought that my time of reckoning with Harald had finally come and he would beat me up.

But he just gawped at me, and by now so many children had gathered around us in the playground that if Harald beat up a girl it wouldn't go unnoticed.

Fortunately, at that moment the gong sounded. Everyone put their empty milk bottles back in the crates. Third period was about to begin and I wondered whether Herr Grashopp really did have a metal plate inside his skull.

*

That was how it started. Then the voice popped up more and more often. It travelled with me across the globe and throughout the whole world as far as Chengdu and Baghdad or Paris, but also anywhere else I wanted to go.

But mostly it would talk to me before I went to sleep, when I'd put *The Time Machine* away and was wondering what the future would be like, since in the book it didn't look as if the future was something to look forward to, even though I didn't understand everything about the story. Actually I understood next to nothing, but I read it all very closely because it had been sent by Auntie Eka, Uncle Grewatsch and Uncle Winkelmann when the time was ripe.

Everyone on the estate looked forward to the future, because life was progressing and would get better and better, they themselves would get richer and richer, and the cars would get more and more horsepower. But having read *The Time Machine* I couldn't shake the feeling that humanity as a whole would just get more and more stupid, and then the accident at the red factory happened.

The red factory was pretty big and everyone who lived on the estate worked there. Our-Uwe and his family didn't live on the estate because he was a departmental manager and had a terraced house where he'd live until he'd climbed a few more rungs on the ladder and would move into a villa just outside town, and my parents didn't intend to grow old on the estate either, but because we came from the East my father had to start at the bottom and work his way up the ladder, so in the meantime we lived on the new estate among people who would never make it to the top of the ladder because from the outset they only did night shifts. That's why Gisela's mother took on cleaning jobs as well, although she had the family treasure in the basement, the chinchillas she'd bought off Herr Reiland and which reproduced like mad, and because of the chinchillas her husband didn't have to make his way up the ladder at the red factory, but could happily work his night shifts on the bottom rung until the family was overwhelmed with riches.

My father couldn't stand Gisela's family because he thought they were pretty stupid. Not quite as bad as Grandma, who was too stupid even to cheat well at canasta, but pretty stupid all the same, because Gisela's mother didn't understand pyramid schemes, otherwise she'd have known at once that Reiland was a crook who'd be living the life of Riley in Switzerland on the 2,000 marks from Gisela's mother and the other fools who'd fallen for his scam.

It's in the name, my father said. The life of Reiland.

She won't see a pfennig for those chinchilla furs. It's her own fault.

My mother couldn't stand Gisela's family either because they ate yellow sausage and had a crate of Frischa in the kitchen and over at theirs you could eat yellow sausage and drink Frischa whenever you liked, and besides they had Formica everywhere. Even the table in their lounge was Formica.

Formica wasn't quite as bad as plastic and elastic because we were in the West, but strictly speaking it was the same thing, just with a different name: in the East it was called plastic and elastic, in the West Formica, which was the opposite of teak, and if someone had Formica, then their children got yellow sausage and Frischa too.

I don't want you going over there, my mother said.

Frischa was the best thing if you were thirsty, and I was usually thirsty because there was a pretty long gap between my school milk at break and the evening. I didn't really believe that you'd get worms from tap water, but you couldn't be sure, so I'd often go over to the neighbours' when Gisela and her sister listened to Elvis while their father slept on the couch and we'd cut out evening gowns and fur coats from the mail-order catalogues that Gisela's mother always got because she didn't want to waste any time putting together the right wardrobe for the bungalow they'd soon have, and I always cut out petticoats because I'd have loved a petticoat, but I'd never get one for the same reason I'd never get a kitten: my mother didn't listen to me when I said I'd love a petticoat, but I could always cut one out, and while we were busy with the mail-order catalogues Gisela's father snored on the couch and we drank Frischa.

Once I asked Gisela's mother about the chinchilla furs, if she had already sold some to Herr Reiland, and she said that the great chinchilla fur auction was about to take place in America. It should have already happened in spring, but something had cropped up in America and so now it wouldn't take place until October, and it would be the biggest auction for luxury furs that the world had ever seen. That's what Reiland had written to her.

Wait, I've got the letter in the kitchen, she said, and went to get it, to show me what a splendid golden letterhead he had, with elegantly curved letters.

Really rather impressive, she said, then read it out to me. Largest fur auction of all time in Ontario. That's in the United States.

Reiland had also written that each chinchilla fur would fetch at least 250 marks.

When you think how the dear creatures are reproducing, she said, smiling.

As far as I know, I said, Ontario is in Canada and not in the USA. On my globe, at any rate, it's in Canada, I added cautiously when I saw the smile freeze on Gisela's mother's face.

Ontario had always been in Canada in Uncle Winkelmann's stories too, and although the light inside my globe didn't work any more and South America was dented, the rest of it was OK.

All of a sudden Gisela's mother's voice went faint. Could someone go and get me the Diercke atlas? she asked, and then the four of us were all bent over the Diercke atlas until Gisela's sister said, well, what do you know? Ontario, Ohio. That must be it.

Her Ontario in Ohio was a tiny dot near Canada, but Germany had places that shared the same name, there was a Frankfurt am Main and a Frankfurt an der

Oder. For my birthday I'd been sent a square record from Frankfurt an der Oder because my uncle had found work at the opera house there. His fiancée had stayed behind in Wallstrasse, like my grandmother, and he'd found a new fiancée in East Berlin and married her, and both had then moved to Frankfurt an der Oder, and sometimes Grandma would write in her letters that she never got to see them.

I checked in the Diercke atlas and found out that Frankfurt an der Oder was quite a lot bigger than Ontario in Ohio, but then again they weren't going to stage an opera there, only a chinchilla auction, and surely they wouldn't need an opera house for that.

All the same, my inner voice told me that Ontario, Ohio, really was a tiny dot on the map, far too minuscule for such a big thing as the largest chinchilla auction in the world, and I thought my father might be right and Reiland had possibly taken Gisela's mother for an idiot.

If they lie to children all the time, I thought, I expect they do it to each other too.

I didn't know what was worse: that they took each other for idiots or that they allowed themselves to be taken for idiots because they simply believed every idiotic thing they were told and didn't want to know where Ontario was.

I was excited about how the auction would go, but in the end I never found out whether Reiland had taken Gisela's mother for an idiot because before that the accident occurred, and then everything happened so quickly, and when things occur that quickly usually you're at a loss afterwards as to what happened, and by the time you understand what did actually happen, it turns out that it was all different. At any rate, one day a car drove through the estate around midday with a loudhailer on its roof.

Ever since the Monte Cassino story, Tassilo had been my friend and we went to school together in the mornings and usually home together at lunchtime too.

He asked me whether it was true that the Nazis had tried to smash the monks' treasures to smithereens.

I said I didn't know for certain, because I couldn't remember everything Uncle Winkelmann had told me, but I thought that it was perfectly conceivable they had, and Tassilo asked Alessandro. Alessandro was his older brother, but he didn't know any more than me and just said that in the end the Italians were pretty angry at the Germans, after having first fought alongside them and the Japanese against the rest of the world. Tassilo's family was both angry and not angry at the Germans. They were not angry because they'd had a really tough time in Sicily and the father had been unable to feed his family, and here in the Promised Land they had a better life, but they were still partly angry because the Germans had enticed the Italians to the Promised Land, and when they came nobody wanted them and nobody could stand them, and so they were only allowed to do the dirty jobs that nobody in the Promised Land wanted to do themselves.

Alessandro had a Solex moped and was almost grown up.

One day he told Tassilo that he hadn't found out any-thing about the treasures, but he had heard that a bear had fought on the Polish soldiers' side at Monte Cassino.

I thought Alessandro was probably at that age where people lie to children all the time.

A likely story, I said.

But Tassilo swore that Alessandro was the only person on earth you could trust. Alessandro would never, ever lie to his brother.

He'd never lie to any of our people, Tassilo said, it would go against his honour, and I thought how I'd love to have a brother like that.

I did have my voice, but I didn't tell anyone about it. Not even Tassilo, and then the accident happened.

You couldn't see the chimney from school, but as soon as we'd crossed into the park from the Liederbach on our way home we saw it, and something wasn't right. The smoke looked different today, even though it was almost as yellow as normal. Normally it puffed out yellow smoke, dark yellow, and from the column of smoke that rose into the air you could tell the direction the wind was coming from. It disappeared somewhere up in the sky, a bit like the white stripes behind the planes, but now it was a little darker than dark yellow and wasn't disappearing; while we were at school it had just come to a standstill where it was in the sky, or at least that's what it looked like, as if it had just stood still and become a thick yellow cloud. We saw it when we went over to the park from the Liederbach. We stopped in the street and held each other's hand, and I didn't care if somebody saw us and blabbed in the playground the next day that we'd been smooching. While we were standing in the street the car with the loudhailer slowly drove past, broadcasting an announcement that everybody should go back home to their houses or flats immediately and stay there until further notice and not leave their houses or flats and close the windows and keep them closed. The announcement had a metallic clang and didn't sound like a human voice. It finished with the words: there is no immediate danger.

That means it's extremely dangerous, Tassilo said. He took me to the front door of our building, and when I got the key out I said, you can come to our flat.

Ever since I'd heard my voice, I'd been saying things I'd never have dared say before.

Tassilo wouldn't have been allowed in our flat, and I shouldn't have said he could come in, because I was not supposed to let anybody into the flat if my mother wasn't there, and my mother never got back from work until much later because we weren't at the same school, and when she came home she was tired and didn't want to discover another horde of children there, happy as she was to have survived the hordes she had to tame at her school, but I thought that the yellow cloud and the announcement might mean that today was an exception.

And if the loudhailer said that we all had to go home to our houses and flats immediately, then it probably meant that we should go to any house or flat on our way home, so perhaps Tassilo and I could go to the same flat rather than to our own homes and make ourselves safe, so I said, you can come to our flat, but Tassilo said, no thanks.

I got the impression that he'd have liked to come in, but maybe his mother had told him that he wasn't allowed to go to other people's flats. He waited until I was inside by the stairs and the door was slowly closing, then he took a few steps back and waved before turning around and continuing on his way.

The cloud grew ever bigger, it stayed up in the sky for a while, then came down slowly, it was a bit like my snow globe, except this wasn't white snow but something yellow. It wasn't flakes either, but a thick mass, and by the afternoon it was everywhere, all the buildings were surrounded by the yellow. By three o'clock the sun could barely break through and it was almost completely dark. My mother had brought home a pile of tests and taken them out to mark, but she didn't get going on them and only then did we realize that the flat had been in darkness for a while now. Sometimes we sat down and sometimes we got up again and peered through the closed windows, watching the yellow stuff settle on the pavement and the road, on the sandpit and the little swing beside the clothes props until they were no longer visible.

I thought the world might be coming to an end. Then my mother said, I really ought to get going with that marking. She turned on all the lights, and just as she was about to mark the first test, long before the cloud started to disappear that evening, Gisela's mother rang at our door. I opened the door and she said there had been an explosion at the factory and she'd just had a phone call to say that her husband had fallen into a vat. A few other men had fallen into the vat as well and after that the yellow cloud had risen out of the chimney and spread all across the sky and then over the ground too.

When my father came home that evening he already knew that Gisela's father and a few other men had fallen into the vat.

My mother said it was a horrible death.

My father said he'd predicted it would happen but Our-Uwe didn't want to listen. Then he said that some heads were going to roll at the factory now.

Poor woman, my mother said. What is that poor woman going to do now?

Then we had supper. I didn't forget to wash my hands, but when we were sitting at the table I said that I wasn't hungry.

Of course you're going to eat something, my mother said.

I heard the voice. It was slightly deeper than mine and very calm.

Like hell you will, it said.

And then I heard myself say, haven't I told you about how I was at Dunkirk?

My parents looked at each other.

I'd found Dunkirk on the globe by chance when I was looking for Ostend, it was slightly below it, to the south of Ostend, not actually in Belgium any more but just over the border, and I thought the name was so beautiful.

I thought Lima was beautiful too, but Lima was in a mountain range that had been squashed into the South American dent on the very first day. I didn't have the courage to walk on squashed land so, in the evenings, when I travelled around the world, I stuck to those areas that were curved, and I was interested in where my grandmother Maria had come from and fled from.

And so I'd stumbled across Ostend, then Dunkirk, but I hadn't told anybody how I'd got to Dunkirk. It was a rainy day and I'd fled Paris, but I didn't want to tell my parents that, because my mother wouldn't have known what to do with me on account of the man I was with in Paris, but obviously she'd have known that it couldn't bode well. I wouldn't say a word to them about the man I'd been so happy in Paris with, but then something happened, we had to separate and I didn't want to be in Paris without him because Uncle Winkelmann had said that Paris was the city of love and you were better off not being alone in Paris, and so in the end I got into my red cabriolet and just drove off towards where it was blue on my globe.

*

107

Towards the sea, I said.

My parents gave me strange looks.

On the way it began to rain. To begin with I'd left the roof open because I found the headwind refreshing, even though dark black clouds were already gathered in the sky and even more black clouds were drifting over from the Atlantic. It looked as if there was going to be a storm. My updo had been blown about and come loose, and eventually I stopped by the side of the road and closed the roof. It bucketed down all the way to Dunkirk.

You couldn't see your hand in front of your face, I said.

Outside on the estate the yellow cloud was gradually starting to disappear, but I wasn't on the estate. I was in Dunkirk and it was four o'clock in the afternoon when I saw the Atlantic Ocean before me. I parked in the harbour because I was hungry and I was certain that the best restaurants would be where the sailors came ashore and wanted a proper meal, a Puszta schnitzel or a Wiener schnitzel, or at least bread with liver pâté and gherkins after months of feeding on dumplings with white sauce, because on the high seas there was nothing else apart from those dumplings day in, day out.

I paused to see the effect the dumplings had on my audience.

My parents had stopped looking at me. They ate and pretended to listen.

And indeed I found one dive after another in Dunkirk. The wind was whipping up so much rain from the sea onto the land that it seemed like the end of the world, but it wasn't at all, the world doesn't come to an end that easily, even though sometimes you might think it will, and then this Chinese man emerged from the misty grey void and came straight towards me. He was on shore leave and far in the distance, invisible in the rain, was his freighter from overseas, with his arm he showed me just how far in the distance, but through the rain I could see only the spray in the harbour and beyond that there was nothing.

In the end I told my parents the whole story about the Chinese man from Chengdu who'd spent months in the engine room of his freighter, into which no ray of sunshine ever shone because the engine room was right down in the bowels of his ship, in the basement actually. It didn't have any windows, at any rate, and although the Chinese man had been given shore leave, there was no trace of sun now either, and of course when he spoke to me I was slightly suspicious at first, because you can't blindly trust every Chinese man who comes your way looking for a dive and just starts talking to you, and I kept going with my story, telling them how we were totally drenched, I kept going up to the point where the Chinese man protected me from a horde of drunken sailors. I hadn't noticed the danger, but he was used to being able to see everything even without light, and he stood in front of me to stave off the attack, it got quite heated and perilous, but he defeated them all with his bare hands. Maybe with the Chinese dagger he had too, because all Chinese men had Chinese daggers. When he'd massacred the lot of them his teeth were grinding with the exertion of it all and eventually the Chinese man and I sat in the dive in the harbour and ate the best prawns in the world.

I'd never felt so sure that the Chinese man, the sea and I were as one, but I decided not to say this because I thought it would be too much for my parents, although I could have said it because my father was tuning the radio to find out whether there was any news about the accident. My mother cleared away the dishes and before she disappeared into the kitchen she said, what will that poor woman do now? She can hardly stay in the flat now, seeing as her husband...

I was sad and thought of the Chinese man who'd never seen the sun, and of the prawn cocktail. During the intervals at the concert in the Centenary Hall everyone used to get a glass of Sekt, and if you wanted you could get some nibbles too. The nibbles were arranged beautifully on a little plate, like the cold cuts Grandma had always served, only in miniature. There were always a few glasses beside the nibbles. They contained prawn cocktail, or at least that's what it said on the label by the glasses, and the prawn cocktail had a pink sauce. I'd have loved to have tried one.

At the start of the summer holidays, Tassilo went to Italy with his parents and elder brother, because his grandad and grandma and uncles and aunts lived there, as well as two big sisters. Tassilo's father had bought a big, old car, because it was a long way and because everyone in Italy was very poor and needed all manner of things they couldn't get there, and although Tassilo's father only did a dirty job in the Promised Land, by the time the summer holidays came around he'd usually amassed so much stuff that he could barely close the boot. Before they drove to Italy Tassilo invited me to their flat.

At first my parents were unsure whether they should let me go to Tassilo's flat, but in the end they did let me go because my father said we'd be getting out of the estate soon and so it didn't really matter.

Just don't make a habit of it, he said as a precaution, and I said that I certainly wouldn't make it a habit.

Before school I packed my swimming things and the annual pass for the outdoor pool into my school bag because it was going to be a hot day. I couldn't fit the towel in; it would have split my school bag.

When I packed my things, the day ahead of me still felt fresh and cool, and like a big adventure, even though I went to the pool almost every day after doing my home-work. But I'd never before packed my swimming things into my school bag before school when it was still cool outside, and it felt as if the packing was the start of a really long journey and that once I'd embarked on this journey I'd go on travelling further and further afield, and never have to come back to our flat.

After school Tassilo and I walked straight past our front door, just like that, as if I didn't live there.

When I gazed at the door it looked completely unfamiliar, and then we walked four blocks further on.

All of the flats on the estate were exactly the same, but inside they were quite different depending on how they were furnished, whether the furniture was made of teak or Formica and whether it matched.

At Tassilo's the furniture didn't match at all, and I decided that when I was bigger nothing would ever match in my flat.

When I took that decision I heard my deep voice chuckling inside me and then it started to laugh. It laughed really loudly.

I'd never heard my voice laugh before and it struck me that I'd never, ever heard a woman laugh before, only the girls in my class who sometimes laughed, but that was more of a giggle.

We had meatballs for lunch, just like at Karlsson-on-the-Roof's, but at Karlsson-on-the-Roof's they were Swedish meatballs without sauce and I'd never tasted them because I'd never been to Sweden, but I knew Karlsson-on-the-Roof from books, and from these books I knew him as if I'd been to Sweden.

The meatballs that Tassilo's mother made swam in a red sauce and smelled like the food in the refugee camp, when the Bulgarian and Romanian women cooked in the communal kitchen, but there I'd been forbidden to taste their dishes, whereas here there was pasta to go with the meatballs too. The pasta tasted of the meatballs with the sauce and we were all allowed to sprinkle cheese on top.

Before lunch I was slightly anxious because I assumed that Tassilo's family would pray. I mean, they were Italians. Italians were Catholics and Catholics prayed before lunch. I couldn't pray because we never did, but in the end they didn't pray, or at least not before lunch. They instead talked about Italy and their grandma and grandpa and all the other relatives. It turned out that their grandma had rabbits too and cooked roast rabbit sometimes, and after lunch Alessandro took me for a lap of honour on his Solex. Then we went swimming and actually it was just like always. A few children from my class were there, and others too who we knew from other forms. Here come the lovebirds, make room, they're going to smooch. Just like always.

But it was also completely different, if only because I wasn't lying on my own towel but one that Tassilo's mother had lent me.

When I got home that evening my mother said, you've been eating garlic. You smell like a gypsy.

Gisela's mother's chinchillas didn't go to Ontario and so I don't know if the auction ever actually happened in that tiny place in Ohio. Gisela's mother wanted to sell them to Herr Reiland because after the accident she had to pay for the funeral, even though the coffins didn't contain Gisela's father or the other men who fell into the vat. The red factory had paid part of the costs, but not all, and after that Gisela's mother got a widow's pension and moved out of the estate because she cleaned part-time and wasn't employed by the factory. Herr Reiland didn't want the chinchillas and, besides, he was going on holiday in July and August, but he wrote that he might be able to take them in September and pass them on to a fur dealer in Switzerland for twenty-four marks.

The fur dealer lived in Lausanne on Lake Geneva and when he took the chinchillas he paid twelve francs. That was less than Gisela's mother had expected and what Herr Reiland had written, but she said, I'm up to my neck in debt, and she had the freight costs to pay too and, just as my father had said, heads rolled at the red factory, and among those heads was the head of Our-Uwe.

And so at the end of that summer we moved out of the estate because my father had climbed a few rungs up the ladder, and on our new estate there were only people who were called *Guten-Tag-Herr-Doktor*, even though my father didn't have a doctorate, just his degree from the East. Virtually all the teak furniture that had been in our old lounge went into my room because they were now buying oak furniture for the new lounge, something my father had decided when my mother started going on again about the larch and her fiancé.

There wasn't a fir-green Opel Admiral either, although we now had a Mercedes, as my father had leaped a few rungs, but for the time being it was only a Mercedes 190 because there wasn't quite enough money for the 600 yet.

At least his youth hadn't gone to waste completely in vain.

That's what he said, at any rate, when we moved into the new estate and my mother had her first parents' evening at the start of the academic year.

When she left he whistled his favourite aria from *Don Giovanni* and got comfy on the couch. 'Là ci darem la mano / Là mi dirai di sì.' I was supposed to get comfy on the couch too, and he said that at least his youth hadn't gone to waste completely in vain, and from now on he was certain that no more of his life would go to waste, and that I was his little mouse and princess.

Eventually he poured himself a submarine. It gurgled, and amid the gurgling I suddenly heard my voice. Or, more accurately, before the voice sounded but while it was gurgling in the glass, I heard the grinding of teeth inside my head and only after that the voice.

There was no laughter in the voice, nor was it in the least bit calm or friendly, but beside itself with anger, such as I'd never heard it before.

It told me what I should do now.

I thought about what I should do now and I became despondent because I would never, ever dare do that.

For a moment the voice said nothing.

My father continued to get comfy and said that he'd really like a divorce now and to enjoy his youth to the full.

My voice was waiting to see whether I'd dare do it or be cowardly.

I curled up and was as quiet as a mouse.

The voice said that now was the time to act, and that you actually know most things and it's your own fault if over the course of time you forget much of what you actually used to know, when you had no idea of all the things you knew, and that's why, the voice said, you need all those books later on. Merely to find out what you actually always knew.

I didn't know if my voice was right.

Then I thought of the three monkeys.

Then I looked at the hands that were sinking the little glass inside the big glass.

Then I looked at my own hands, which of course weren't burnt and covered in rubbery growths, because I hadn't got trapped in a fire by accident whose flames almost weren't put out in time.

Then I took the glass from my father's hand and flung the contents in his face.

Du dommen jong, I said, went into my room with the old teak furniture and closed the door.

I moved to a new school. Gisela and her sister didn't know where we'd gone and I didn't know where they'd gone, so I couldn't visit them, and when I said that I wanted to visit Tassilo my mother said that the people on the old estate weren't our sort of people any more. And that's why we didn't go to the Schwanen now either.

The Italians like to keep to themselves, my mother added.

Just like the people in Wallstrasse, I thought.

But I didn't believe her.

Although I'd moved to a new school I still took the bus when I went to Isolde Ickstadt's friend's for my exercises, only now it was the number 32 rather than the 11, but that didn't make much of a difference. On the 32 it was just like on the 11: the Russians had their eye on our carpets and young girls, they were standing right on the border of their sector, just waiting to drop their atom bombs on us. Someone had to show the Greeks how to wash and if the Eyeties hadn't stabbed us in the back we wouldn't have the Yanks over here now, ruining our young people. If there were no young people on the bus, then everyone always looked at me, even though I was only seven years old rather than a young person, and then I heard about all the things that would happen to me. The American chewing gum would rot my teeth, soft-serve ice cream would make me fat and I'd get 'negro babies' from Elvis Presley.

I didn't believe that I'd get a 'negro baby' from Elvis Presley. Sometimes I thought about the time machine and wondered whether, as it said in the book, we really would all go gaga in the future, but the time came when I didn't have to take the bus any more because I'd lifted enough marbles with my toes at Isolde's friend's and hopefully my legs were now long enough, and that evening I looked at the globe to see all the things I could do with my legs that were the same length. Isolde Ickstadt had said that I could go skiing and dance rock 'n' roll and turn boys' heads, and while I thought about which of those three I wanted to do, my deep voice came to my aid. I listened very carefully.

Let's begin gradually, it said, one thing after the other.

I spun the globe a few times and didn't know exactly where one thing after the other would begin.

It's quite simple, the deep voice said. You just have to remember the future.

I thought that this probably had something to do with the time machine, but I didn't know what.

What do you think of Switzerland? the voice said after a longish pause, and immediately I remembered once having a birthday and going skiing with my friends.

Lausanne is in Switzerland, on the globe it's at the top of Lake Geneva, in the middle. Lake Geneva isn't actually called Lake Geneva, but I already knew that because Dunkirk isn't called Dunkirk, and Lake Geneva is actually called Lac Léman, which was in brackets beneath it. I liked the name. It clatters when you say it out loud and sounds a bit like Lima, but Lima is in the dented mountain range where I didn't fancy going, the lake looks like a banana and on the other side of the lake, opposite Lausanne, is where the Alps begin. On most mountains there's snow all the time, even in summer, something I knew from Uncle Winkelmann's books, which had pictures of the Alps with and without skiers, and from Lausanne they're only a stone's throw away.

In the mornings I just had to take the bus into town, where I'd skip school, because you don't learn anything at school anyway. Every child knows that, but nobody knows that every child knows it, so everyone thought I was going to school and that's why nobody noticed. Instead of going to school I went into town, to cafés, to the cinema, or went to the mountains with friends, and of course the mountains were covered in snow, but there were no people other than my friends and I. We carried our skis on our shoulders and trudged through the deep snow, which was mostly blown in drifts by the wind. You had to be careful not to sink into the drifts and suddenly disappear, seeing how deep they were. Hour after hour we trudged uphill, my friends always ahead, because they were students already and could go skiing or to the cinema whenever they wanted, but they took me with them, even though I was still pretty small, a long way from being a student, and was skipping school. All this climbing was making me very hot, the skis were heavy on my shoulders, but I couldn't stop because the others were going on ahead without turning around, and if I hadn't kept up with them they would have lost me. Besides, I didn't want to stop because the sky was blue and the sun was shining on the snow and there had never been anything more beautiful than being here in the world and so I kept trudging on while every bone in my body ached.

When I got thirsty I stuffed a load of snow in my mouth, because there's nothing better than snow when you're thirsty, and it won't give you worms either. You don't even get worms from tap water, you needn't believe everything they tell you, and finally we'd reached the

top. My friends had said that this was the most beauti-
ful mountain on earth. Even more beautiful than the
Matterhorn. I'd seen pictures of the Matterhorn in Uncle
Winkelmann's books, and of course I'd thought that the
Matterhorn was the most beautiful mountain there was,
though I'd never been there.

Now I was standing on this one here, and indeed
it was the most beautiful mountain on earth. Luckily
there wasn't any edelweiss on this mountain. Uncle
Winkelmann had told me that no edelweiss grew on the
Matterhorn either, someone had faked them into the
pictures he had in his book about the Alps, and luckily
there wasn't any edelweiss on this mountain either, so
nobody would have an accident trying to pick one on
the steep rock face. The whole thing took a long time,
but finally we'd reached the top.

At the top there wasn't much space for all of us,
because it was a real mountain peak, and no sooner had
we reached the peak and were scrambling to get a view
of all the neighbouring mountains around us and the
land with the lake far, far below than my friends, one
after the other, began to push off and ski down. One by
one they kept pushing off and skiing down, and when I
tried to see where they'd gone, they were already far away
and nowhere to be seen, until the last person pushed off
and skied down.

After that I was alone on the peak, thinking that I
should push off and ski down now too, but I didn't know
where, because on every side there was a vertical descent,

no sign of a piste or path, just snow, in which I could no longer see traces of how we'd got up here.

I unfastened my skis and sat down to think.

The lake was very far down and very far away. Even though I was seeing it from above it didn't look like a banana, as it did on the globe, but of course the globe was just a globe and not reality.

In reality it looked like a big pond, and when there were no clouds drifting above it, it was as blue as the sky, but sometimes clouds gathered and covered the sky and then it was black.

But it was very far away, right in the distance, even though I knew that it was actually quite close because I'd be taking the bus after school this evening and the bus stop was on the promenade by the lake. Down by the shore it looked like a lake with lots of colourful sailing boats on it.

Only from up above did it look like a pond.

I fastened my skis again, because I didn't want to stay up at the top when it turned dark and freeze during the night.

Then I got frightened because I didn't know how to get back down.

At some point I finally found a place from where I could ski vertically down the mountain, and I pushed off, and when I got to the bottom I wasn't singing as loudly as when I'd set off, but I was still humming the birthday song, and my friends were laughing when they saw my wet face that was bright red and half frozen, and

I laughed too because the song had echoed so beautifully off the steep rock face at the top, and I'd got here and found them again, even though I couldn't have known that as I skied down, and I hadn't known.

And how I'd sung.

I'd sung, I'm so happy! as loudly as I could, travelling so quickly that the air had swallowed the other half of the line. I couldn't even hear it myself, but when I got to the bottom and turned around, it was as if it were still hanging up above.

Subscribe

Discover the best of contemporary European literature: subscribe to Peirene Press and receive a world-class novella from us three times a year, direct to your door. The books are sent out six weeks before they are available in bookshops and online.

Your subscription will allow us to plan ahead with confidence and help us to continue to introduce English readers to the joy of new foreign literature for many years to come.

'A class act.' GUARDIAN

'Two-hour books to be devoured in a single sitting: literary cinema for those fatigued by film.'

TIMES LITERARY SUPPLEMENT

A one-year subscription costs £35 (3 books, free p&p for UK)

Please sign up via our online shop at www.peirenepress.com/shop

BASMEH & ZEITOONEH
RELIEF & DEVELOPMENT

Peirene is proud to support Basmeh & Zeitooneh.

Basmeh & Zeitooneh (The Smile & The Olive) is a Lebanese-registered NGO. It was established in 2012 in response to the Syrian refugee crisis. B&Z aims to create opportunities for refugees to move beyond being victims of conflict and help them to become empowered individuals who one day will return to their own country to rebuild their society. Today the organization is managing nine community centres in the region: seven in Lebanon and two in Turkey.

Peirene will donate 50p from the sale of this book to the charity. Thank you for buying this book.

www.basmeh-zeitooneh.org